Presented To:

_____

From:

_____

Date:

_____

ONE SEASON
OF HOPE

JIM STOVALL

Sound Wisdom

P.O. Box 310

Shippensburg, PA 17257-0310

Cover design by: Kelly Morrison, Eileen Rockwell

For more information on foreign distribution, call 717-530-2122. Reach us on the Internet: www.soundwisdom.com.

ISBN 13: 978-0-7684-0712-9

ISBN 13 Ebook: 978-0-7684-0713-6

For Worldwide Distribution, Printed in the U.S.A.

1 2 3 4 5 6 7 8 / 18 17 16 15

Greetings:

I want to thank you for taking the time to explore the first book/movie title in my new Homecoming Historical Series. Each book and movie in the Homecoming Historical Series will combine elements of an inspirational novel with a historical retrospective.

Other book/movie titles anticipated in this series include:

The Will to Win—
A Tale of Humor and Perspective from Will Rogers High School

Making Your Mark—
A Story of Wit and Wisdom from Mark Twain High School

Top of the Hill—
A Saga of Wealth and Success from Napoleon Hill High School

The Making of a King—
An Adventure in Tolerance and Forgiveness from Martin Luther King, Jr. High School

The Building of a Dynasty—
A Novel of Champions and Victory from John Wooden High School

Each of these book/movie titles and others to follow will appeal to my existing audiences including businesspeople, success-oriented readers, the faith-based community, public and private schools, and readers around the world who love inspirational novels as well as a relevant historical perspective.

I look forward to exploring the possibilities with you.

ONE SEASON OF HOPE

The first novel/movie in the new Homecoming
Historical Series by bestselling author Jim Stovall

*When you think you have nowhere to go, no one
to turn to, and no way out, you've still got hope.*

CONTENTS

INTRODUCTION

by Jim Stovall

MY DEAR READER, YOU HONOR ME GREATLY WITH YOUR investment of time and money in this book. I take your investment seriously and am committed to doing everything in my power to insure that your investment pays off for you.

I have written 25 books that have sold millions of copies in dozens of languages. At this writing, five of my books have been turned into movies. Every time someone spends their hard-earned money and valuable time with my message, I am both humbled and grateful.

I have written books that contain the wisdom of prominent people, books that tell inspirational stories, and books that share thoughts and ideas of my own. This title contains elements of all three. Within these pages, you will learn about the wisdom, thoughts, and deeds of President Harry S. Truman; you will meet some compelling and inspiring fictional characters from Truman High School; and be exposed to my thoughts and perspective that will, I trust, make it all relevant.

I owe a great debt to Dennis Giangreco, award-winning Truman author and historian. Dennis invested his valuable time to insure that my vignettes of President Truman within these pages remain accurate and consistent. After you finish this novel, I'm hopeful you will want to learn more about President Harry S. Truman. In that event, I enthusiastically refer you to D.M. Giangreco's titles *Dear Harry* and *The Soldier from Independence*.

This story—which will, hopefully, make it to the movie screen—is the first in my series of books/movies within the *Homecoming Historical Series.*

Several years ago, there was a popular movie entitled *Back to the Future.* In this book and the entire *Homecoming Historical Series,* we will learn how to go forward into the past. I have long believed in the powerful phrase, *If we do not learn from our past, we are destined to relive it.*

Harry S. Truman himself often said, "Not all readers are leaders, but all leaders are readers."

One of my movie partners coined the phrase, "If you can tell a great story, you earn the right to share your message." Within this book, I hope you not only enjoy a great story but learn from the wisdom of Harry S. Truman and find a perspective that will allow you to apply those lessons in your personal and professional life.

As always, I remain committed to your success. Any time you don't feel these principles apply to you or you just need some encouragement, I can be reached at Jim@JimStovall.com or by calling 918-627-1000.

I'm looking forward to your success.

Jim Stovall, 2014

Chapter One

MILESTONES AND MEMORIES

*"There is nothing new in the world
except the history you do not know."*
—HARRY S. TRUMAN

1

I N THIS LIFE, THERE ARE OCCASIONS THAT HAVE BEEN VIVIDLY imagined and eagerly anticipated for years, but even so, their impact can never be fully calculated. In that surreal moment, I found myself seated on the dais next to the podium in the cafeteria at Harry S. Truman High School.

High school cafeterias across the country inevitably look, sound, and smell the same, but with a few balloons, a bit of glitter, and some tired streamers, these cafeterias can be magically transformed into an exotic prom setting, a solemn graduation venue, or—in my case—a retirement banquet hall.

The crooked banner hung above the dais proclaimed, "Happy Retirement Coach Fullerton." My name is, indeed, Glen Fullerton, but for the last 42 years within the Truman High universe, I have simply been known as Coach.

Harry S. Truman High is located in an unremarkable town which comprises our quiet community known as Springfield, but in its own way, Truman High is a universe unto itself.

During my own high school days in this very building, I often dreamed of exciting adventures in faraway, exotic lands. I wanted to see, taste, and feel the whole world. As I looked out over the enormous crowd gathered for my retirement banquet and saw the faces of all the people who have become my family, I realized that I've been everywhere, seen everything, and done it all without leaving home.

Seated below me at long rows of tables that stretched into the distance like ocean waves approaching the shore, I saw the young boys, middle-aged men, and a few senior citizens who comprised the clay with which I sculpted my life. It seemed no more than the blink of an eye since I had been a student and an aspiring football player in this very place.

Every morning for the past several years, I gazed into my bathroom mirror and saw an old man looking back at me. The lines etched in my face vividly attested to each of my 66 years on this earth.

One of the cheerleaders who was filling the role of waitress for my retirement banquet that evening had set a plate of food in front of me shortly after I sat down, but mercifully, I never got the chance to eat it. The cafeteria food at Truman High can be best described as predictable and consistent throughout the 45 years I ate my meals there as a student and then a teacher and coach.

That night, there was the inevitable mystery meat artfully concealed by some form of gravy, flanked by tired and wilted vegetables that had been boiled within an inch of their lives. But my dinner that evening remained untouched as a steady stream of Truman Eagles, young and old, stood in line to approach the dais to offer their greetings, congratulations, and thanks.

I think of these former players as my boys. Whether they are 18 or 60, they will always be defined in my own mind as "my boys." I will always think of them as they were the first day they came to me as excited, scared, and anxious boys hoping to be one of the chosen young men who received their own coveted Truman High Eagles football jersey.

That night, there were business leaders, war heroes, and the governor of our state waiting their turn to have a word with me along with plumbers, carpenters, cab drivers, and others representing virtually every path one could take in this life. But that night, we were all together once again to celebrate our shared experience as simply Truman High Eagles. I greeted them one at a time. Their history, accomplishments, and contributions to our world make up the fabric of my life.

Coaching football does very little to change the world. I never cured cancer, solved world hunger, or put a man on the moon, but I realize in some ironic way I helped to mold the young men who made their mark in each of those areas and many more.

My outstretched hand was firmly grasped in a warm and vibrant handshake, and I felt the steady, unwavering gaze of those piercing brown eyes belonging to Rob Wakefield. Robert Garrett Wakefield, Esquire, is known across the country and around the world for arguing the most complex and intense cases before the Supreme Court of the United States. He strikes fear in the hearts of judges and fellow litigators alike, but to me, he will always be remembered as the slowest, smallest, and clumsiest guard who ever showed up for that first day of practice. Nothing stood between him and being summarily cut from the team other than his constant intensity and unwavering tenacity.

On that very first day of practice, on a 100-degree, mercilessly-humid day in mid-August, Wakefield demonstrated a talent for absolutely nothing except the ability to trip over his own feet and everyone else's on the practice field; but somehow, on the last day of practice when we had to cut the squad down to our final roster, he got the very last jersey.

I was hopeful that his work ethic and energy would somehow rub off on the more talented players that year. But then, slowly and inevitably, he began to work his way up the depth chart and actually got to play in a few games. By the end of that season, due to some unfortunate injuries, I was forced to spread some players around the field, and Rob Wakefield actually became our starting right guard. Although he had made a lot of progress that season, he still tripped a couple of times getting in and out of the huddle.

We needed to win that particular game to make the state playoffs that year, and as time wound down in the fourth quarter, I knew it was going to be really close. I'm certain several of the deepest wrinkles in my face originated during that very game.

Then it was fourth and goal on the two-yard-line, and we needed a touchdown to cap off our winning season and move into the playoffs. Otherwise, our season was over, and we had the long winter's wait 'til next year.

When you're only two yards away from the goal line, it doesn't seem like much of an obstacle, but we had started that series after a great punt return, first down and goal, on the one-yard-line. The ensuing three plays had netted us a one-yard loss, and that simple two yards seemed like an unimaginable gulf.

I called an end-around play because our previous three hand-offs into the middle of the line had achieved less than nothing as we were moving backward. I knew if we could get our speedy halfback around the corner, we would score and win. The only thing that stood in our way was the opposing team's defensive end who hadn't performed particularly well that night.

As our team broke the huddle, I was confident and somehow knew that my innate coaching prowess would get us the victory. But my counterpart across the field displayed his own coaching prowess as he shifted the defense. I instantly realized that the play I had called involving our best offensive lineman pulling to block their mediocre defensive end allowing our speedy halfback to get around the corner had gone up in smoke, and now their other defensive end who was an All-State performer destined for the state university stood between us and the goal line, and the only blocker we had on that play would be Robert Garrett Wakefield.

Having no timeouts left, I was forced to rely on every coach's last resort. I prayed.

As our quarterback took the ball from the center, everything seemed to move in slow motion. He turned and deftly handed the ball to our speedy halfback who raced toward the sideline, cradling the ball in his right arm. Their All-State defensive end looked 12 feet tall and solid as the Great Wall of China as Wakefield stumbled down the line.

Every coach learns that players cannot be measured simply by height and weight. There are certain intangibles that enter the scene at the most unexpected times. Just when everybody in the stadium, including me, was certain that Wakefield would be brushed off like an annoying gnat, and our halfback would be crushed by their defensive end, a collision took place and somehow their All-State defensive end destined for the state university and the NFL found himself flat on his back with Truman's own Robert Garrett Wakefield lying atop him as our halfback scampered into the end zone.

I never saw Wakefield trip, stumble, or even hesitate after that play. Somehow, in the blink of an eye, he had transformed into the man who stood before me at the retirement banquet that night.

I proudly proclaimed, "Rob, we're all proud of you and everything you've done since your days here at Truman High." I thought of him standing before the Supreme Court and said, "I really don't know how you do it."

He waved off the compliment and said some nice things about me.

Then, just as he was moving away, he whirled and asked, "Coach, do you remember..."

I smiled, nodded, and assured him, "How could I ever forget?"

Anyone eavesdropping on our private moment would have been baffled by our exchange, but I knew what he meant, and he knew that I knew. Those are the moments that bind us together forever.

I reveled in the next few minutes, enjoying similar fond memories with many of my boys until a somewhat self-absorbed, pompous gentleman from the school board walked to the podium and began tapping on the microphone. He took a sheet of paper from his jacket pocket and unfolded it on the podium. In a monotone voice, he droned on as he read the prepared statement recounting the statistics and accomplishments that made up my life.

Then he mercifully stopped talking and sat down, and I was greeted with a thunderous standing ovation as I approached the podium. As I gazed out over the sea of faces that each held a special place in my heart and soul, I waited for the applause to die down. As the room fell silent, I hoped that my mind and voice would not fail me.

In an almost disembodied way, I heard myself say, "Thank you all for being here and sharing this special night with me. As Truman High Eagles, we have enjoyed winning seasons, we've suffered losing seasons, we've celebrated a few championship seasons, and we've even experienced one season of hope."

Chapter Two

POSSIBILITY AND POTENTIAL

"The buck stops here."
—HARRY S. TRUMAN

2

SOME PEOPLE BELIEVE THE YEAR BEGINS ON JANUARY 1ST. OTHERS think it starts on the first day of school. They would all be wrong. The new year officially begins on the first day of football practice.

I will never forget the first time I walked onto the grounds surrounding Harry S. Truman High School. I was 15 years old and scared to death.

Beginning high school marks one of those life transitions that take us from the top of the heap to the bottom of the barrel. I had gotten used to being the proverbial big man on campus at the local junior high school but now was starting over once again.

The official school year would not begin for several weeks, but I had arrived that morning at Truman High for my very first high school football practice. I had confided to my grandfather that I was a bit intimidated about the transition to high school and, particularly, going out for the football team. As was his custom, he paused thoughtfully and then said, "I don't know much about it," which was always his preamble to saying something brilliant and imparting wisdom. He continued, "I never played high school football, but if it were me, I would get there early, keep my mouth shut, and do what I was told."

I found it to be solid advice on that occasion as well as many other occasions over the next half a century.

Having heeded my grandfather's advice, I was walking across the empty high school parking lot more than an hour before the practice was scheduled to start. All the doors were locked, and I could only find one lone figure in front of the school sweeping the sidewalks around a statue.

As I approached the man with the broom, I couldn't help but notice he was talking to himself. Even after he saw me approaching, he continued his one-sided conversation. I was already nervous, and this made me even more uncomfortable, so I employed the universal mask that all scared teenagers use, and I acted cocky, flippant, and disrespectful.

I laughed and said, "Hey, can you stop talking to yourself long enough to tell me how to get into the locker room for football practice?"

He stopped sweeping, turned to face me, and stared directly at me for what seemed like an hour but probably wasn't more than a few seconds.

Finally, he replied with dignity, "I am Rufus McCoy, the head maintenance engineer for everything in and around Harry S. Truman High School." Then he continued with a question. "And you are?"

I stammered and stuttered and finally croaked out, "Glen Fullerton."

He smiled warmly and stated, "It's nice to meet you, Mr. Fullerton, and for your information, I wasn't talking to myself. I was conversing with the president."

I must have appeared bewildered because he took that opportunity to gesture toward the statue that I later discovered was a life-sized image of Harry S. Truman, himself.

Mr. McCoy went on to explain he would unlock the doors to the gym and locker rooms precisely a half hour before practice, so I had at least 20 more minutes to wait.

I inquired sheepishly, "Do you really talk with the statue?"

Rufus McCoy rumbled out a laugh that made his wrinkled ebony skin attest to his long life and many years of service to Truman High and answered, "Well, I wouldn't say we converse as much as we communicate."

I asked, "What do you communicate about, and do you really talk to him like Truman?"

Rufus McCoy pondered a moment then explained, "We talk about important things and current events. We've been in touch with each other for going on 40 years. I used to call him Mr. President, then Mr. Truman, but now we're pretty much down to Harry and Rufus. You might say we're on a first-name basis."

Little did I know then that Rufus McCoy would become one of my best friends, and I would take up his dialogue with Mr. Truman that would stretch out for the next 40 years of my life.

I actually made the team that year but mostly warmed the bench, but by my junior year I got to play quite a bit of football, then made the starting squad my senior year.

I learned a lot from old Coach Bartlett those three years. I learned a little bit about football and an awful lot about life.

I had no way of knowing on that first day that after graduating from Truman then spending four years at a teachers' college, I would be right back at Truman as Coach Bartlett's assistant for two years; and then after his retirement banquet I became the head coach of the Eagles, which would be my role for the next 42 seasons.

It all started in my fifth year as the head coach. I wasn't even 30 years old yet, but I felt like I had a good handle on my team and on my life. Sometimes you just don't know what you don't know.

Harry Truman was fond of saying, "It is understanding that gives us an ability to have peace. When we understand the other fellow's viewpoint, and he understands ours, then we can sit down and work out our differences."

On a hot day in August, I greeted my returning players and welcomed the new boys. I gave them my standard head coach speech involving hard work, being a part of the team, and the fact that we were all Eagles whether we made the varsity or not.

Then I turned the team over to the assistant coaches so they could begin running drills with the various position players. The offensive line gathered in one end zone near the blocking dummies; the defense spread out across the midfield area; and the quarterbacks, receivers, and running backs assembled in the far end zone. I made my way to the top row of bleachers on the 50-yard-line to survey our prospects for the coming season.

Most people think that football is about competing against another team, but from the opening practice until the season starts, it's really about competing against other players to make the team and get a starting position.

Harry himself may have said it best. "In reading the lives of great men, I found that the first victory they won was over themselves...self-discipline with all of them came first."

Each year, a few of the sophomores will make the varsity squad, but most of them will spend their first year or two on the junior varsity which is a place for boys to go who aren't ready for primetime and may never be.

My most difficult role at the beginning of each season is filling the roster to the limit and then being forced to cut boys who didn't make the team. The hardest part of this is dealing with the seniors. Some of them have struggled for two years on the junior varsity but now, in their senior year, they either make the varsity team or turn in their jersey.

On the first Friday night of September in little towns across the country, the stadium lights shine brightly, and a drama unfolds that is literally a part of Americana; but many hours of hard work and much blood, sweat, and tears have to be expended before those young men can take the field in front of their friends, family, schoolmates, and hometown.

August practice seems chaotic when it begins. More than a hundred puzzle pieces are randomly scattered across the table, but through the ensuing days of practice, a lot of the pieces start to fall into place, and a picture of a football team begins to emerge. Unfortunately, as the first game of the season approaches, some of the puzzle pieces don't fit and have nowhere to go. These are the boys whose hopes and dreams are not going to be realized on a football field.

As I sat at the top of the bleachers day after day, juggling the puzzle pieces in my mind, I spotted several top prospects who would be high school stars, and I even identified a few young men who might have a college career in front of them.

The majority of the boys on the field would make our team that year but probably would never be more than average high school football players. And then there were the outcasts and misfits. Some of them had just come out for the team as a lark. Once the hard work began, they usually quit long before I was forced to cut them. Then there were the inevitable aspiring ballplayers who wanted it badly, and they were willing to work hard and sacrifice, but they had simply not been blessed with the God-given talent to be athletes.

It was during the final week of practice before the season began that year that I noticed another figure seated in the bleachers down near the end zone on about the third row. As I thought about it, I realized he had been there for several other practices, and I became curious. I had met most of the boys' fathers but didn't recognize the stranger watching our practice taking place on the field below him. I wondered if he could be a scout or an assistant coach from one of the teams we would be playing in the coming weeks. Eventually, my curiosity got the best of me, and I walked down the stairs and took a seat next to him.

I offered him my hand and stated, "I'm Coach Glen Fullerton."

He nodded and answered, "Steve Ryan."

The suspicion came through in my voice as I demanded, "So are you an opposing coach, a scout, or just a spy?"

He sighed thoughtfully and replied, "I'm a doctor."

I had confronted him to get a few answers but found myself facing more questions.

Finally, I asked, "Well, Doctor Ryan, do you have a son playing on my team?"

He shook his head timidly and mumbled, "No, just a patient."

A million thoughts raced through my mind, and I blurted out, "Doctor, is there something I need to know about one of my players?"

He stood up, turned to face me, and said, "Yes, there is."

Then he turned and walked away, leaving me sitting in the bleachers confused and baffled.

My assistant coaches and I were gathered around the scarred and battered conference table in the athletic office on the final Saturday before the first game. Each player's name had been written on a card, and they had been divided into groups and placed in order of talent and skill so we could make the cuts necessary to create our final team roster for the season. As the head coach, the final decision was mine, and I tried to do the right thing for our team and each boy represented by one of those cards.

The starting players' names had already been filled in on our depth chart. The backup players' names had been written beneath each of the starting players' names, and we were down to the last few slots to fill. My assistant coach called out the names as he turned over the last few cards.

"Lawrence."

"Cut," I replied.

Then he read, "Garrett."

"Keep him," I responded.

We were down to the last slot on the team with four cards to go. My assistant turned over the next card and asked a question that will be etched in my heart and soul for the rest of my life.

"What about Bradley Hope?"

Chapter Three

HOPE AND FATE

"If you can't stand the heat,
get out of the kitchen."
—HARRY S. TRUMAN

3

FOUR ASPIRING, EAGER YOUNG MEN COULD NOT FIT INTO ONE football jersey. I mentally arranged the four players in order of talent and benefit to the team, then I rearranged them over and over, but it always came up the same way. Bradley Hope was at the bottom of the list with three players between him and making the Truman Eagles for his senior year.

I probably never had a player with less talent and more heart than Bradley Hope. It seemed inevitable, and it was only six days before the kickoff of the first game, but I looked at my assistants and declared, "Let's table it for now and look at it again on Monday."

The sun was fading in the western sky as I walked out of the school building that Saturday night. Without really being aware of where I was going, I walked straight to the statue of Harry S. Truman and looked up at that great and historic man. During Harry's time, a lot of people thought he was undersized and lacked talent, but he became the most powerful man in the world and changed history.

I thought about the decision Harry had made to drop the atomic bombs on Japan in hopes of saving a million U.S. soldiers' lives. It felt a bit ridiculous to be standing there struggling with the decision to cut a few boys from a high school football team, but somehow I knew that Harry would know how I felt and share my anguish.

I tried to make it a habit to keep Sundays set aside for church, family activities, recreation, and relaxation, but that next day I continued to be haunted by the vision of the cards with players' names scattered across the conference table in the athletic office. The cards read Mills, Stevens, Slade, and Hope. No matter how much I wanted them to appear in a different order, my mind wouldn't let me do it.

I owed my team, my integrity, and my memories of Coach Bartlett nothing less than the best players possible on that season's roster.

Monday morning found me in my customary setting seated at my desk in the U.S. History classroom at Truman High. Being a coach was my passion. Teaching history was my profession.

Both of these pursuits were part of my inheritance that Coach Bartlett had left me as his legacy. It began on my first day of class as a student at Truman. I was wandering the halls, looking at the building map and classroom schedule that had been given to me as I arrived for the first day of school.

I stumbled into U.S. History for second hour as indicated on the papers and was shocked to find Coach Bartlett seated behind the desk at the front of the classroom. I had come to know him over the previous few weeks as a hard-driving, demanding coach out on the football field, but there he was in a jacket and tie, looking like a history teacher.

More to impress a cute blonde girl standing next to me than anything else, I loudly greeted Coach Bartlett as if we were old comrades.

"Hey, Coach, if you have any really tough history questions, just ask me."

All the other kids laughed, but I couldn't quite read Coach Bartlett's reaction, so I was a bit apprehensive that I might have stepped over the line.

After everyone found a desk and roll was called, Coach stood and announced, "My name is Mr. Bartlett, and we will be learning U.S. History this year in this class."

Coach Bartlett took out his textbook, and all of the students followed suit in anticipation of the first lesson.

Coach looked at me, seated on the fourth row behind the cute blonde, and said, "Before we start today's formal lesson, I would like to pose a question to our very own Mr. Fullerton."

All eyes shifted to me, and Coach continued.

"Mr. Fullerton, would you please rise and prepare to dazzle us with your grasp of history."

I heard chuckles and jeers throughout the classroom. I slowly stood, preparing for the worst.

Coach spoke. "Mr. Fullerton, as this is our first day of history class at Harry S. Truman High School, what would you say if I asked you what the initial "S" stands for in President Truman's name?"

I was hoping the floor would open up and swallow me, or we would have a sudden power outage or even a fire drill that might get me out of this crisis.

Coach prompted, "Mr. Fullerton, what would you say?"

I mumbled, "Sir, I would say nothing."

The laughter throughout the room was interrupted by Coach Bartlett responding, "You're absolutely right, Mr. Fullerton. Quite impressive."

I was as baffled as the rest of my classmates as I couldn't imagine how having nothing to say was the right answer to a question. If there was anything said during that next hour comprising our first U.S. History lesson, I was unaware of it. I sat there, stunned and confused.

Eventually, I realized that the bell had rung, and everyone had gathered their books and were making their way out of the class except for me.

I jumped up and prepared to rush out when Coach Bartlett intervened saying, "Not so fast, Mr. Fullerton."

I slowly lowered myself into my seat and tried to imagine what horrible fate awaited me.

He continued, "By this time tomorrow, you will research, prepare, and write a two-page essay on why your answer—'nothing'—was correct."

His demeanor went from teacher to head coach as he demanded, "Do we understand one another, Mr. Fullerton?"

That was the spark that lit the fire that became a burning, lifelong fascination and love of history in my life.

Old Harry often said, "If you can read this, thank a teacher." It's one of the many things in my life for which I remain grateful to Coach Bartlett.

After football practice that night, I rushed home, determined to get my two-page essay on Harry S. Truman completed. There was only one good thing about this entire dilemma. My beloved aunt, Alva Lea, who had always been a special influence in my life, had given me a gift when I was 12 years old. I didn't appreciate the gift when I received it, but that night, it seemed like a life preserver for a drowning young man. Aunt Alva Lea had the greatest spirit and best attitude of anyone I ever met. I have often thought, if I could have put my aunt's spirit into a linebacker's body, we could have rewritten the football record books.

Alva Lea lived in Kansas City, Missouri during the years President Truman was retired and also living in the area. When Truman completed his two-volume memoir, my Aunt Alva Lea somehow arranged to get a first-edition copy for me, signed by the former president. Today, it remains one of my most prized possessions and holds a place of honor in my trophy case.

Thanks to Truman's memoirs, I found out that Harry's parents each wanted his middle name to be in honor of a relative on their individual side of the family. Apparently, the debate went back and forth until Harry's mother and father both realized that each of the relatives whom they wanted to name Harry after had a name beginning with the letter "S." From that moment forward, he was known as Harry S. Truman, and, indeed, the "S" actually stood for nothing.

That Monday morning, I greeted the students and slipped comfortably into my role as their history teacher. I gave them my stirring first lecture of the year and left them their assignment for the week involving writing their own essay on the life of President Harry S. Truman, requiring them to include what the "S" stood for within their essay.

Teaching is a rigorous profession, as not only do you have to keep the students' interest and attention, but you have to repeat the same lesson several times every day to the various classes that you are teaching.

Throughout that morning, my mind seemed to wander back to the cryptic conversation and mystery surrounding Dr. Steve Ryan. A quick Internet search revealed that his office was less than two miles from Truman High, so I decided to commit my one-hour-and-10-minute lunch period that Monday to solving the mystery of Dr. Ryan.

I rushed into his waiting room and approached the young lady at the counter, stating, "I have an emergency and need to consult with Dr. Ryan."

She glanced down at her schedule book and asked, "Are you the radiologist or the surgeon?"

As I headed purposefully down the hall toward where I assumed Dr. Ryan's office would be, I explained, "Ma'am, I'm a football coach on a mission."

At the end of the hall, I did indeed find Dr. Ryan seated behind his desk which was piled high with charts and files. He was unwrapping a sandwich he obviously intended to have for lunch. He waved me toward a chair as the receptionist rushed in behind me exclaiming, "Doctor, I'm sorry... This man doesn't have an appointment, but I couldn't stop him..."

Dr. Ryan smiled reassuringly and said, "That's okay, Judy, I forgot to tell you about his appointment, and I think he would be rather hard to stop anyway."

Judy seemed bewildered but nodded and retreated back toward her counter and left me with Dr. Steve Ryan.

There was an uncomfortable silence between us which he broke by saying, "As a physician, I'm recommending to myself that I don't eat this entire pastrami sandwich." He looked over at me and continued, "Do you want half?"

I nodded, and he slid half the sandwich across the desk toward me, perched atop a paper towel.

We ate in silence for a few moments, and he finally explained, "Coach, we doctors deal with certain standards, oaths, and confidentiality rules."

I nodded in understanding and said, "And we coaches deal with certain responsibilities involving knowing everything we can about each player so that we can help boys have fun while they are turning into young men."

He nodded in understanding and seemed to weigh the matter. Finally, he dug through some files on the edge of his desk and opened one in front of him. He glanced through several sheets of paper, leaned back in his chair, and directed a powerful gaze at me.

He let out a deep breath and said, "Coach Fullerton, medicine is part art and part science. The trick is to be applying the right one at the right time. I'm going to employ a bit of art and a bit of science and assume that I can trust you."

I nodded emphatically, and he continued.

"It's Bradley Hope."

"What about Bradley Hope?" I asked.

He glanced down at the paperwork in the file and continued.

"It is my best guess that this will be Bradley's last year."

I was confused and stated the obvious.

"Of course this will be his last year. He's a senior."

The doctor shook his head and explained mournfully, "I don't mean his last year at Truman High. I mean his last year here."

The doctor waved his arm in a circular, all-encompassing motion that told me everything I needed to know and more than I wanted to know. He did his best to help me understand something called Ewing's sarcoma. He assured me that Bradley would be safe to play football this coming season but probably wouldn't be alive a year from now.

I blurted, "Doc, it may seem trivial to you, given the situation here, but I've been struggling with my own dilemma regarding Bradley. He is, without a doubt, one of the greatest kids I've ever been around, and he's a true joy to work with, but my roster only has one opening left with four players in contention, and Bradley Hope is the smallest, weakest, slowest, and least-talented football player among the four."

The doctor looked at me with alarm and said, "Is there anything you can do? I've been treating Bradley for six months, and the only thing that's keeping him alive, and the only thing that means anything to him, is to be a Truman Eagle this football season."

I leaned back in the chair and stared at the ceiling. Finally, I pointed out the obvious.

"Doc, it looks like we both are in a bad spot."

He looked at me and said, "Coach, I'm open to suggestions."

I answered, "Doctor, when you've thought of everything you can and you've done all you know to do, it's time for The Eagle's Edge."

Chapter Four

QUESTIONS AND ANSWERS

*"I come to the office each morning and stay
for long hours doing what has to be done
to the best of my ability. When you've done
the best you can, you can't do any better."*
—HARRY S. TRUMAN

4

I LEARNED ABOUT THE EAGLE'S EDGE FROM OLD COACH BARTLETT which is where I learned much of what I know that has made me who I am. It was during my first year as his assistant coach, and it was late in the season. We were trying to claw our way into the last berth in the playoffs and were playing one of our arch rivals, then and now, the Granite Ridge Giants.

If I had looked at it realistically, I would have admitted that they were a better team than us. Fortunately, coaches never have to be realistic.

We had played really well and were only five points behind late in the fourth quarter. Unfortunately, Granite Ridge had the ball, and they seemed to be willing to just run out the clock, but during a simple hand-off to their halfback, they fumbled, and our defensive tackle out-fought everybody for the football.

There was under a minute to go, and we had no more time-outs. Coach Bartlett had been forced to use up all of our timeouts early in the second half when we couldn't get the right players on the field and get them lined up correctly. This always guaranteed Coach B would be in a bad mood.

With time running out, we tried a couple of pass plays to the sideline so at least our receivers could step out of bounds and stop the clock. We got to their 40-yard-line with eight seconds to go. This would be our last play, and we had to have a touchdown.

Football fans around the world call it a Hail Mary pass. It's the last-ditch, final-chance effort that involves the quarterback simply dropping back and throwing the ball into the end zone in hopes that his receiver will catch it, or there will be a pass-interference penalty resulting in one more down.

Coach Bartlett signaled the play, then turned to me and stated emphatically, "Glen, we've got this."

I expressed my doubt and tried to point out that we were 40 yards from the end zone, and on his best day with a vigorous tailwind, our quarterback might pass the ball 30 yards.

Coach Bartlett responded confidently, "Then it's time for The Eagle's Edge."

I must have looked bewildered and confused, because he continued, "When you've thought of everything you know and have done everything you can, you've just got to believe that your best is good enough."

Our quarterback got the snap and dropped back to throw the Hail Mary pass. Our receiver raced down the sideline, heading for the end zone with their best defender matching him stride for stride. They were the only two on that side of the field except for an out-of-shape referee trailing the play by a few yards and trying to get into position.

As our receiver approached the goal line, the quarterback reared back and threw it for all he was worth, but as I had feared, it was obvious to me and everyone in the stadium the pass was going to fall short of the end zone; but then, The Eagle's Edge took over, and the ball bounced off the referee's head, cleared the defender's outstretched arms by a fraction of an inch, and nestled into our receiver's hands as he tumbled into the end zone.

The crowd erupted in thunderous cheers as I stood openmouthed, staring at a semi-conscious referee sprawled on the four-yard-line, their frustrated defender who had landed on his back at the goal line, and our receiver in the end zone holding the ball as confused as everyone, trying to figure out what had happened.

Coach Bartlett turned to me, clapped me on the shoulder, and proclaimed, "Glen, that's The Eagle's Edge. You can use it whenever you need it."

It was Friday, and later that night was our first game of the season. By 4:00, we would need to have our roster set, pass out the game jerseys, take the team photo, and get ready for the game.

That morning, I beat everyone to school and approached the president hoping he could provide some inspiration. I explained to him that I felt like there was a right thing to do and then there was a good thing to do. He listened patiently—Harry was always a good listener—but he didn't have much to add to that situation.

I remembered his struggles with the labor unions. The same unions that had gotten him elected in 1948, Harry believed, were choking the life out of the country. He felt as if he owed his loyalty to the unions, but he owed his allegiance to the people of the United States. Harry did the right thing, which made him unpopular with the unions and in some other circles, but he went down in history as a man who pursued his principles and never looked back.

After a difficult decision, Harry often said, "I shall continue to do what I think is right, whether anybody likes it or not."

He paid a price for his principles, which may have been what prompted him to declare, "Want a friend in Washington? Get a dog."

I taught all of my classes that day, and in mid-afternoon, I headed down the hall for the athletic office. On opening day of any other football season, I would have been totally focused on the game, but as I turned on the light in the conference room, the four cards with players' names on them confronted me from just where I had left them on the table.

I scooped up the cards and sat down at the head of the table. I spread the cards out before me like some sort of real-life game of solitaire. Each of those cards represented the hopes and dreams of a young man as well as his friends and family. There were memories to make, games to win, and opportunities to be gained or lost.

At 3:30, my equipment manager stuck his head in the conference room and announced, "Coach, I've got all the jerseys in the boys' lockers just like you assigned them on the roster."

He glanced down at a crumpled piece of paper and continued. "But there's one name missing... Who gets the last jersey?"

The future hung in the balance, and I delayed the inevitable as long as possible, replying, "Just leave it here with me."

He shrugged, tossed the jersey on the table, and left.

As I was weighing what I wanted to do against what I needed to do, compared to what I should do, I realized it was time for The Eagle's Edge.

Just then, the phone rang at the other end of the conference room. Eventually, it became apparent that no one else was going to answer it, so I walked the length of the room and picked up the receiver.

After I mumbled something, the voice on the line said, "Coach Fullerton, this is Harriet in the principal's office. We just got a call from the hospital. Apparently, Steve Mills fell down the stairs this morning before third hour. It seems he was paying more attention to one of the cheerleader's skirts than the top step, and he went all the way to the landing. The nurse who called said his ankle's broken, so I thought I ought to let you know."

I thanked her, hung up the phone, walked back to my chair at the head of the table, sat down, and slid the card with the name *Mills* on it toward me. I looked at it for a moment, picked it up, crumpled it into a ball, and sank a three-point shot into the trash can in the corner of the conference room. What had seemed insurmountable had dwindled down to merely impossible.

Then I heard a persistent tapping on the doorframe. I glared toward the intruder interrupting my intolerable task, ready to chew out one of my players when I realized it was Tina, a student worker in the school office during sixth hour. She approached with fear and trepidation, and I smiled, trying to allay her anxiety.

She reached out a shaking hand and gave me a memo and squeaked, "It's from the principal."

She turned and rushed out of the conference room, leaving me with three cards on the table and a memo.

Memos from the principal's office generally involve some type of inane paperwork or archaic expense voucher requests. It was my standard practice to ignore these entirely as anything of importance would elicit a phone call or a visit from the principal, but having stared at the remaining cards as long as I could, I picked up the memo and read: *Coach Fullerton, we just got the paperwork from Rick Stevens' mother informing us that she is being transferred by her employer out of state, so her son is withdrawing from school immediately.* The principal had signed it with his illegible scrawl.

I picked up the card that read *Stevens*, crumpled it up, and hit my second three-point shot of the afternoon.

I could hear the players excitedly streaming into the locker room to get their new jerseys and get ready for the big game that night. There were just two cards lying on the table before me. I felt I was so close but still so far away.

Without preamble, Eleanore Drumright swept into the room and confronted me. Mrs. Drumright had been my world literature teacher just a few years before. I struggled through her class the entire year and emerged with a newfound love for literature and poetry, along with a hard-earned C on my report card. I always took solace in President Truman's statement, "The 'C' students run the world."

Mrs. Drumright and I were now fellow members of the faculty, and her classroom was across the hall from mine. Eleanore had done a better job than I had managing our relationship from student/teacher to colleagues. I didn't know whether to greet her as Eleanore, Mrs. Drumright, or simply *Yes, ma'am.*

She declared, "Coach Fullerton, we've got to talk right now."

I sighed and replied, "Mrs. Drumright, I've got a lot on my plate right now... Can it wait?"

She continued as if I had not spoken.

"It's Kevin Slade."

Mrs. Eleanore Drumright—teacher, colleague, and friend— had my full attention. I jumped up and held a chair for her, and we sat at the conference table together.

She began. "Kevin Slade failed my literature class last year."

The spark of hope I had momentarily felt extinguished as I nodded and explained, "Eleanore, I know all about that, but Kevin made up that English class this summer."

Mrs. Drumright slapped a blue-lined essay book on the conference table in front of me and declared, "This is the result of Mr. Slade's efforts in summer school."

I beckoned her to continue, and she said, "He was to write an essay on *Dante's Inferno*."

I nodded and asked, "So what's the problem?"

She jabbed a finger at the essay book and exclaimed, "I asked for *Dante's Inferno*, and he gave me a few undecipherable paragraphs on the Chicago fire."

I clapped my hands together and began chuckling. Mrs. Drumright leaned forward and glared at me, proclaiming, "Glen Fullerton, I know that some teachers and most coaches don't take world literature seriously, and they think football is all that matters here... Well, I'm here to tell you today that my class is important, and Kevin Slade is getting another F, making him ineligible for football or anything else this year."

I assured Eleanore that world literature was vitally important to me. In fact, I told her I could honestly say that it had taken on an elevated importance in my estimation that very day.

I held the chair for Mrs. Drumright and walked her to the doorway, thanking her for upholding high standards for our students, Harry S. Truman High School, and Dante himself.

I scooped up the cards that read *Slade* and *Hope* and dropped them into the waste basket, silently thanking Coach Bartlett in the process.

I picked up the last game jersey for that season and walked into the locker room. Players were excitedly putting on their new jerseys and getting ready for the game as I made my way along the third aisle of lockers to the end of the row where I spotted Bradley Hope seated on the bench in front of his open locker. As I got closer, I could see the tears running down his face.

I startled him when I put my hand on his shoulder, and as he turned to me, I experienced one of the great privileges in my

42-year coaching career as I held out the jersey and announced, "Son, this is yours."

Chapter Five

BEGINNINGS AND ENDINGS

"A pessimist is one who makes difficulties of his opportunities, and an optimist is one who makes opportunities of his difficulties."
—HARRY S. TRUMAN

5

It was less than two hours until the kickoff of our first game that season, but I was still in the athletic office. It had taken so much focus, effort, and energy to complete our team roster for the year, including Bradley Hope, that I hadn't given our game plan the usual intensity I bring to each contest. Thankfully, we had a home game to open that season, so I just had to walk through the school grounds, across the parking lot, and into the stadium.

My players and the assistant coaches were already over at the stadium, going through preparations and warm up, but I had one more detail to complete before I could join them.

I picked up the phone and dialed. I heard a voice I recognized announce, "Dr. Ryan's office."

I said, "Judy, this is Coach Fullerton. You may remember me. We met the other day."

Judy stuttered and stammered but obviously remembered who I was. She finally composed herself and asked, "Sir, how can I help you today?"

I responded, "Well, I need to talk to Doctor Ryan."

She chuckled and said, "I'm assuming this is another emergency?"

I laughed and explained, "Well, Judy, to be honest with you, I am a bit pressed for time, and there are a lot of people waiting on me."

"Hold on," she said efficiently, and after a few seconds of elevator music, I was greeted by Dr. Steve Ryan.

"Good afternoon, Coach."

I began, "Doc, I've got a bit of an update on our boy. I'll start with the bottom line, and we can fill in the details later... Bradley Hope is an official member of the Truman High School Eagles football team this year. He has received his game jersey and is at the stadium, preparing for our opening game as we speak."

There was a long pause, and Dr. Ryan asked awkwardly, "Coach, did you have to...?"

I interrupted and assured him, "Doc, it was a straight-up, legitimate deal. I owe everyone involved, including Bradley, too much to do anything less than put the best people on the roster."

"How did you do that?" the doctor asked. "Didn't you have several players ranked above Bradley for the final spot?"

I thought about it a minute and realized I couldn't understand what happened myself, much less explain it to Dr. Ryan, so I took a different approach.

"Doctor, do you ever have a patient who's hopeless, and even though you've done everything you know how to do, it's not enough, but somehow they get better?"

Dr. Ryan answered tentatively, "Yes, that happens on very rare occasions."

I continued. "Well, doc, what do you call that?"

He sighed loudly and replied, "Coach, it's kinda hard to define, but I guess it's just a medical miracle."

"That's it," I shot back. "I think we just had a football miracle over here."

I thanked the doctor, told him we would stay in touch, and let him know there would be tickets and sideline passes for him for the game that evening. I hung up the phone and looked down at the battle-worn conference table that a few hours earlier had held four cards representing young men and now was clean and clear.

I rushed out of the building and headed for the stadium. Even though I was far later than I had ever been for a game, much less an opening game of the season, I had to pause for a moment to exchange some thoughts with the president. I looked up at the statue and could almost swear he had a contented look on his face as if he somehow knew that Bradley Hope had made the team, I had fulfilled my responsibility while maintaining my integrity, and we were about to kick off a new season.

I spoke aloud. "Well, Harry, I won't bore you with the details because I think you already know what happened. Sometimes new beginnings come in the most unlikely ways. It's kind of like when you were a relatively unknown senator from Missouri and you were selected as President Roosevelt's fourth vice presidential running mate."

I paused and glanced around the vicinity to make sure no one was eavesdropping on my conversation with the president. Somehow I felt that if people saw me talking to a statue, it probably wouldn't do my reputation or Harry's any good.

I continued, "FDR had been president so long and had switched vice presidents each term, so most Americans didn't know who you were before or even after he put you on the ticket, and you weren't even the first or second choice, but then after the election the unthinkable happened, and in the blink of an eye, you became President Harry S. Truman."

I glanced at my watch and realized, although I was really late, I felt confident my assistant coaches could handle the pre-game routine, and I could take a couple more minutes to finish my thoughts with Harry.

"Even after you became president and you were instantly thrust into the biggest game in a brand new season, there were more changes to come. You hadn't even settled into the chair behind your desk when Pentagon officials came into the oval office to tell you that they had harnessed the atom, and the world had entered a new age that you had never heard about."

I guess life brings us a lot of new beginnings, and a few of them come with unexpected and unanticipated surprises.

I said my goodbye to Harry, and I knew he would be following the progress in the game that would be starting shortly in the stadium just across the parking lot.

A lot of people would probably think it strange that a coach and history teacher would carry on a dialogue and a friendship with a deceased historical figure. After knowing Harry all these years, I think it strange everybody doesn't do it.

I rushed into the stadium which was rapidly filling up with parents, students, marching bands, cheerleaders, reporters, and fans. I paced the sideline watching my team go through their last few drills before they would head back into the locker room where they would be until the game started.

The plays were crisp and clean. My team looked enthusiastic and ready to play without seeming too overly emotional. A team has got to be mentally prepared and intense without being out of control.

I watched each player in each position perform their pregame routine. Every team is different, and every year is a clean slate. The plays may be the same, and the Xs and Os on the chart remain constant, but the boys who make up those various positions on the board are different every year and even grow and develop from game to game.

The team I was looking at, that moment, was not the team I had finished the season with last year, but this team would be different in the next few weeks than they were on that opening night.

My assistant coaches looked to me, and I nodded, signaling that we were ready. Whistles blew, and the players rushed into the locker room and sat on the benches and the floor, making a circle with an opening at the end of the room. That was my spot.

The pregame speech to the team is a time-worn tradition. Some people think it is a bit cliché, but I can assure you it matters. People are both physical and mental. The strongest and fastest teams don't always win. A great mental attitude and motivation can make up for a lot that may be lacking in an athlete.

I took it seriously because I knew these boys would remember this moment for the rest of their lives. I can quote some of old Coach Bartlett's speeches that happened decades ago as if I just heard them.

I waited for the room to fall silent, cleared my throat, and began.

"Gentlemen, there's been a lot of hard work and preparation that's brought us to this point tonight. I'm proud of each of you for being here. We began this season on the hottest days of August and practiced two and sometimes three times a day. We pushed you hard, and I know some of you stretched yourselves beyond where you thought you could go, but here you are tonight, a part of the Truman High Eagles tradition.

"A lot of great people have worn that jersey before you, and a lot of aspiring young boys will be coming after you. It's important that you don't let any of them down.

"Once we go out that door and run onto that field, there will be a lot of things we can't control, but the two things we can always control are our effort and our attitude."

I let my gaze roam across the faces looking up at me, and I knew I had their full attention, then I made eye contact with Bradley Hope sitting cross-legged on the floor in front of me as I continued.

"Football is a game, but there are habits we form and lessons we learn that will carry us through the rest of our lives. Winning becomes a habit just as losing becomes a habit. If you do anything less than your best, you not only let the guy next to you down, but you make it easier to be mediocre again next time."

I looked at each of those eager young men and felt pride for who they were and who they would become.

I concluded, "The talking's over. Let's go do what we came here to do."

The Eagles exploded into a roar of excitement. They clapped and high-fived one another. I moved to the door that opened into the tunnel that led under the stadium and onto the field. I put my hand on the door but looked behind me one last time at those very special young men. When I knew it was the moment, I nodded at them and shoved the door open.

Different people are put on this earth for different reasons. For some individuals, there is no higher calling than being a parent, a carpenter, a banker, a pilot, or an accountant. Each of those professions require dedication and devotion. There are certain poignant moments in every human endeavor that epitomize who we are and why we're on this earth.

For a parent, it might be standing by and watching their child as they take their first step. For a police officer or firefighter, it might be that once-in-a-lifetime opportunity to save someone and make a difference. For a football coach like me, it's the privilege of molding boys into young men, and it culminates in the act of leading them onto the field. I had the honor of doing that 42 times for the opening game of a new season. For me, it was as close as I ever got to heaven while still on this earth.

Chapter Six

WINNING AND LOSING

*"It is amazing what you can accomplish
if you do not care who gets the credit."*
—HARRY S. TRUMAN

6

I HAVE EXPERIENCED FOOTBALL AS A FAN, A PLAYER, AN ASSISTANT coach, and a head coach. Each perspective creates a bit of a different view of the game.

As my team rushed onto the field amidst the fanfare and thunderous cheers from the opening-day crowd, I looked across the field at our opponents for that game. We faced the Plainview Warriors every year during the time I played and coached at Harry S. Truman High School.

Plainview is a little town, much smaller than Springfield, located about 40 miles away. They were not considered a major rival of ours and, frankly, could not compete with us most years. During the many decades I played and coached at Truman, I think we got beat by Plainview less than five times. They were a smaller school from a smaller town that somehow didn't seem to have the collective competitive spirit that surrounded Springfield and Truman High School. Their players were generally not as well conditioned as ours, and I hoped they weren't nearly as well coached.

My team huddled around me and took a knee at the edge of the field for a final word before the kickoff. I reminded them of the new plays and formations we had put in this season and cautioned them about fumbles and penalties. I repeated what I had been telling them all week about our opponents.

"If we play our best and they play their best, we should win this game tonight." I directed my gaze around the players kneeling before me and continued, "But don't ever forget, if we let down our guard and they have some early success, we could lose our opening game to these people. That would ruin many of the goals and plans we all agreed on for this season."

A lot of coaches lie to their teams, trying to convince them that their opponent is stronger than they are, but I always expected my players to tell the truth, and I wanted them to know that they could expect the same from me.

Our team had voted on a captain from our offensive players and one from our defensive players. Our tradition at Truman High was that these two captains would select a third player to serve as a captain for each game. I was very pleased and quite surprised when they told me that Bradley Hope would be the special team captain for that opening game.

Our two regular captains and Bradley Hope walked out to midfield for the coin toss. As I looked at them, I was struck—once again—by how small Hope was but how much energy, enthusiasm, and life he exuded.

I had told the captains that if we won the coin toss, we wanted to kick off. Many coaches want the ball first, but I believe, when playing a lesser opponent, if you can kick off and hold them in the first series, forcing them to punt, you can create momentum and great field position.

The referee introduced our three captains to the three Plainview Warrior captains and flipped the coin. As the visiting team, the Plainview captain called, "Heads," and the referee announced that it was tails. Bradley Hope confidently declared that we would kick off, and the teams took the field.

Every year, a coach gets a new crop of players. You never quite know what you've got until the first game comes around. You can have some positive indications or experience some disappointing trends during pre-season practice, but it's all just a theory until the ball is teed up and kicked off for the opening game. It's a little like trying on a winter coat in a department store. It may look good in the mirror and feel like it would be warm while you are in the store, but you really don't know what you have until the wind blows on that first cold morning.

I thought it was a positive omen when our kicker, who had never kicked the ball beyond the 10-yard-line in preseason practice, put the opening kickoff well into Plainview's end zone, eliminating their opportunity to run it back and forcing them to begin play on the 20-yard-line.

Our defense, which had seemed fairly quick and tough during scrimmages against our own team, proved to be dominant in that opening series against Plainview. Our defensive line stopped them for no gain on their first two running plays, and then our defensive end sacked their quarterback before he could throw a pass on third down, leaving Plainview facing fourth down and 16, which forced them to punt. Their punter shakily caught the snap and barely got off an anemic punt that trickled out of bounds at Plainview's 40-yard-line.

Our offense took the field for its first series of the new season, already well into Plainview territory. We had, indeed, established momentum and created great field position. Good players make coaches look smart.

Some players perform well in practice but freeze up during games. Other players go through the motions in practice but come alive when the stadium lights up on Friday night.

Jessie Hunter was our quarterback that year. I thought he would be an above-average player based on his performance in the preseason workouts, but when he took over the team to direct them down the field in that opening game against Plainview, I felt like I had an All American on my hands. He threw two pin-point passes that each went for major yardage and got us down to their 8-yard-line. Then, on an option play, Hunter faked a hand-off like a magician and ran into the end zone on his own.

I was the one who had called that play, but looking back, I would have to admit that even I hadn't realized he had kept the ball himself until he crossed the goal line.

The Truman Eagles continued to exceed my expectations on both sides of the ball throughout that first half, and we headed into the halftime locker room with a comfortable 21 to 3 lead.

My halftime routine varies based on the score and how my team is playing. When your team is playing well, you just want to congratulate everyone and encourage them to keep the fire going. When things are not going well and there's no fire to keep going, it's the head coach's job to light a fire. I think some of the great instantaneous attitude adjustments through-out recorded human history have occurred in halftime locker rooms, initiated by disappointed and angry coaches whose teams were not performing.

On the opening game that season, I felt that everything was rolling along quite nicely at halftime, so when I went into the locker room, I slapped a few backs, passed around a few well-tar-geted compliments, and left it to my assistant coaches to go over specific plays and elements of the game plan we would implement in the second half.

I had five or six minutes before I would need to give my half-time speech to the team, so I stepped out of the locker room to stretch my legs and get a bit of fresh air.

A Friday night football game in a small town is a lot more than 22 boys playing a game on a field. It is a time when a whole community comes together to become reconnected, reinvigorated, and show its pride.

Most people who know me would be shocked to learn that I love to watch marching bands during halftime. I always admired the precision that those kids displayed on the field. I knew that many hours of practice had gone into each of their routines.

I've never been sure why in our society some people are more admired than others simply for what they do and not just how well they do it. This phenomenon is already evident during our high school years as a mediocre quarterback becomes the hero while an outstanding clarinet player goes unnoticed.

Harry once observed, "Men often mistake notoriety for fame and would rather be noticed for their vices than not be noticed at all."

As the Truman High marching band left the field, the cheerleaders took over, performing their acrobatic routines. In many cases, the best athletes in high school are not on the football field, the baseball diamond, or the basketball court. They are the cheerleaders on the sideline.

I watched a young lady perform a twisting back flip and land on the shoulders of two other cheerleaders to form a pyramid. I just stood there in awe realizing that there wasn't one boy in my locker room who could have done that.

I spent another minute soaking in the atmosphere then realized it was time to give the Eagles a quick pep talk and kick it off for the second half.

As I turned toward the locker room, I felt a tap on my shoulder and looked around to see one of the cheerleaders standing there. I thought her name was Gina, but I wasn't certain.

She shyly inquired, "Coach, is Bradley Hope going to get in the game during the second half?"

I shrugged and replied with one of my standard head coach statements, "We'll have to see. We just take it one play at a time."

Just as my hand touched the doorknob of the locker room door, I heard the familiar voice of Ralph Schaefer. Ralph is the head sports reporter for our local hometown newspaper, *The Springfield Herald*. I was certain Ralph had to be the head reporter because he was the paper's only sports reporter.

He called, "Coach, just one minute."

Ralph rushed over, out of breath, but continued, "Since you've obviously got this game in the bag, can you go ahead and give me a postgame quote so I can make my deadline?"

This was a time-worn ritual that Ralph and I went through for years.

I feigned frustration and replied, "Ralph, you and I both know your deadline's not until midnight, and you just want to get me to say something so you can rush in to your editor to get your story in first so you can beat Mary Ann Bledsoe and her society article so you'll have a few extra column inches tomorrow."

Ralph nodded and shrugged, replying, "Coach, a guy's gotta do what a guy's gotta do."

I shook my head emphatically and stated, "Ralph, you know as well as I do that it isn't over 'till it's over, and anything can happen in a ballgame. If I give you a postgame victory quote right now, as sure as the school board wants to cut my budget, we will lose this game, and you and I will both have egg on our faces in the morning."

Ralph nodded slowly, but I continued, "Please don't make me remind you about the 1948 election when our beloved Harry S.

Truman himself was in a tough campaign, and some idiot from the Chicago paper jumped the gun with that famous headline, *Dewey Defeats Truman.*"

Like me, I'm sure Ralph was visualizing that famous image of Harry grinning from ear to ear, holding up the paper with that infamous headline. Harry won that election just like I knew we were going to beat the Plainview Warriors, but I wasn't going to take the chance.

Ralph's interruption had almost made me late for my half-time pep talk, but he had given me the inspiration for what I was going to say. I told the boys about that reporter in Chicago in 1948 who had assumed the contest was over before it was done, thereby going down in history forevermore connected to that *Dewey Defeats Truman* headline.

I paused to look at each of my players scattered around the locker room and closed my speech with, "Now, let's get out there, finish strong, and end this thing right."

As I resumed my place on the sidelines for the second half, I saw Dr. Ryan approaching me from the bleachers.

He shook my hand warmly and said, "Coach, I didn't want to interrupt you while you were working, but I wanted to check on our boy."

I looked around and saw Bradley Hope sitting on the bench next to the cheerleader who had talked to me at halftime.

I turned back to Dr. Ryan and said, "Doc, Hope was really excited to get his jersey and make the team, and even though we're ahead and a lot of guys are going to get to play, Hope is the last guy on the roster, and I doubt if he gets in tonight."

Dr. Ryan nodded and asked, "Who's the young lady with him over there?"

I shrugged and said, "Like you, I think she's just curious whether or not he's going to get to play."

We continued to dominate the Warriors in the second half. Bradley Hope and three other boys did not get to play in that game at all, but Bradley was a tremendous asset to the team. He was in motion all the time, yelling, cheering, and encouraging every player on the team as they came off of the field. It's easy to be enthusiastic and motivated when you're on the field of battle, but when you can be a positive force on the sideline, you become a secret weapon for the team.

I felt that all of our hard work and preseason preparations had paid off. I knew that the team might be better than I thought, and as I watched Jessie Hunter playing quarterback, I realized this year could possibly be really special.

There were all of the postgame celebrations on the field and in the locker room after that game. A lot of reserve players had gotten into the game, getting some valuable experience, and we had still come out on top 35 to 10. I reveled in the feeling of victory as the players, one by one, stowed their gear, dressed, and left the locker room to enjoy the rest of their Friday night.

My thoughts were interrupted when the locker room door banged open, and I heard cleats walking along the corridor into the locker room. I looked up to see Bradley Hope approaching me. I was about to comment on our big opening win, but I could see that he had something else on his mind.

Bradley Hope walked right up to me, poked me in my chest, looked up into my eyes, and demanded, "Coach, I need the answers to two questions."

Generally, I would not allow a student or player to treat me disrespectfully, but I felt this was a special circumstance. I just nodded and let him continue.

He demanded, "First, I saw my doctor talking to you on the sideline. Did he tell you about my condition? And second, did I really make this team, or did you just feel sorry for me?"

Chapter Seven

LOVE AND WAR

"There isn't any doubt that a woman would make a good president. They make good senators, good members of the House of Representatives, and have held other important offices in the government of the United States."
—HARRY S. TRUMAN

7

THERE I WAS IN THE LOCKER ROOM UNDER THE STADIUM AT Harry S. Truman High School. Just a few minutes earlier, that same locker room had been filled with dozens of excited young men who had just won their first game of the new football season.

I thought about all of the triumph, tragedy, joy, and heartbreak that had unfolded over the years in this one locker room. I knew there had been a lot of stress, tension, and challenging moments, but I was certain that none of them compared to the crisis I felt as I faced Bradley Hope and his two immense questions.

President Truman himself had said, "Tact is the ability to step on a man's toes without messing up the shine on his shoes."

I had always treated my boys the way I wanted to be treated, so there was nothing to do except launch into it.

"To answer your first question, Dr. Ryan did tell me about your condition."

Bradley slammed his fist against the lockers and groaned in frustration.

He blurted, "No one was supposed to know. I just wanted to have the best year I can have, and I wanted everyone to leave me alone."

I nodded, understanding his feelings but felt I had to get through to him.

"Son, we're not just a team. We're a family here. Are you telling me that if something was wrong with me and I was facing a challenge, you wouldn't want to know?"

He spluttered, "Well... I just..."

"Well, nothing," I interrupted. "I saw Dr. Ryan sitting in the bleachers day after day during preseason practice. I thought he was a scout or a spy from another team."

Bradley broke the tension as he laughed, and I joined him and continued, "When I confronted the guy, he told me he was one of my player's doctors, and I hope you can understand that there are times, if you're going to be who you need to be, you have to learn what you don't know."

Bradley Hope nodded, and I went on. "I confronted Dr. Ryan in his office, and he reluctantly and cautiously told me about your situation."

Bradley shot back, "I thought doctors were supposed to be confidential."

I nodded in agreement and added, "Well, mostly they are, but in the first part of the oath they take, they have to commit to doing no harm. I think Dr. Ryan discovered that it would do more harm to not tell me than to tell me."

Bradley Hope nodded reluctantly, and I continued, "Son, Dr. Ryan trusted me, and I hope you will do the same."

The silence stretched out between us, and I determined to wait him out. High school football players can be very stubborn, but their patience is no match for a coach who's seen a few more football seasons than they have.

Finally, Bradley Hope spoke. "So, did you know about my cancer when you decided to put me on the team?"

I hate times in life when lying seems more comfortable and convenient than telling the truth. It's like my grandfather used to tell me about fishing lures. The brightest, shiniest ones have the sharpest hooks. If Bradley Hope deserved anything, he deserved the truth, so I explained, "I knew about your diagnosis several days before I decided who would and wouldn't make the team this year."

Bradley mumbled, "So I didn't really make it fair and square."

Now it was my turn to react. I punched the lockers against the wall near me, pointed my finger directly into Bradley Hope's face, and declared sternly, "Son, if you've learned anything about me during your sophomore and junior years, you know that if I say something—good, bad, or ugly—that's the way it is. So I'm going to tell you flat out, once and for all, you earned the last slot on the roster for this year's football team."

Bradley Hope nodded tentatively, wanting to believe what I was saying.

I pushed on. "I figure it's bad enough to have to deal with cancer. You don't need somebody feeling sorry for you or lowering the bar so you can make it. You got your position on the Truman High Eagles this year because you were flat out the best player I had at the time to complete our roster."

I fixed my gaze on him and finished with my best argument.

"And finally, son, do you think I would cheat one of your teammates out of his place on the team because you were going through some difficulties?"

Bradley shook his head slowly. Then a smile of satisfaction broke across his face. I patted him on the back and put my arm around his shoulder, and we began walking toward the door.

I said, "For two guys who just won their first game of the season, that's about all the time we ought to spend yelling at one another tonight."

Bradley Hope agreed.

We walked out of the locker room and emerged into the cool night air. It had still been hot and humid during the ballgame, but we could feel the cool air settling in as we moved toward the parking lot.

Near the edge of the stadium lights, I could see two small figures standing beside the path that would take us out of the stadium gate.

As we approached, Bradley called, "Hey, Mom, great game, huh?"

A small, frail woman stepped forward and hugged Bradley.

I prided myself on knowing my players, their families, school grades, and everything else that makes up a teenaged boy. I remembered that Mrs. Hope was a single mom working two jobs to try to make up for Bradley's deadbeat father who had disappeared.

Bradley said, "Mom, you know Coach Fullerton."

She gave a weary smile, nodded, and said, "Good evening, sir."

I responded, "Ma'am we're sorry to keep you waiting. Bradley and I had to clear the air on a few issues."

Mrs. Hope quickly turned to Bradley, asking, "Does he know?"

Bradley put his hand on his mother's shoulder to keep her from saying anything else as he gestured toward the other figure emerging from the darkness.

He called, "Hey, Gina. Don't just stand there. Come over and congratulate the coach on our big win."

The other small figure emerged from the shadows revealing the cheerleader who had asked about Hope and had sat with him on the bench.

As a football coach and history teacher, I may not be the swiftest when it comes to interpersonal relationships, but even I could see the special connection between Bradley Hope and Gina.

She offered a timid, "Hello, Coach, and congratulations."

I thanked her and complimented her on her cheering and the acrobatic stunts she performed.

"Gina, if I could get my wide receivers to run and jump like you, we would definitely make it to the state championship this year."

We all laughed.

Bradley stepped beside Gina as they slowly walked toward the parking lot, and I fell in next to Mrs. Hope.

Bradley's mother whispered, "Coach, I don't know where to go, what to do, or who to tell…"

I sighed and tried to sound reassuring. "Mrs. Hope, Bradley's a good boy, you're a great mother, and we're all in this together. That's going to have to be enough for now, and we'll just take it one step at a time."

I felt her small hand squeeze mine, and then she rushed to join Bradley and Gina. They all called, "Good night," to me and disappeared into the darkness, leaving me standing alone to contemplate all that had happened and everything that the future had in store.

I crossed the empty parking lot and walked directly over to President Truman. He was only a shadow against the star-filled sky. I told him how insignificant winning or losing a game seemed compared to life and death.

I was reminded of when Harry was challenged by the Ku Klux Klan, and they threatened his life. Harry's wife, Bess, had just given birth to their daughter, Margaret, and the KKK's malignant threats seemed more ominous as Harry considered his growing family.

I spoke to him. "I know you were scared, and you had to be confused about what to do, but being you, you dealt with them head-on."

Harry had decided to confront the Klan at one of their large meetings in Lee's Summit, Missouri. Bess—and Harry's best friend, Eddie Jacobson—begged him not to go as Eddie had a lot of experience with the Klan. He was one of the things they hated most. Eddie was a Jew.

For the rest of his life, Harry treasured his relationship with Eddie Jacobson and knew that his friend was giving him sound advice; but on that occasion, Harry took the bull by the horns.

The Klan meeting fell silent when they saw that Harry had walked in on them. Harry defiantly strode to the front of the gathering and emphatically told them if they wanted to kill him, they should just take their best shot right then and there. When none of them responded, Harry called them cowards and berated them. I'll always remember his final jab at that loathsome group.

Harry said, "My friend, Eddie Jacobson, told me that he didn't know who started your organization, but it must have been a Jew because only a Jew could sell you idiots a $1.98 bed shirt for $16.00."

The KKK members sat in stunned silence.

I admitted to Harry, "Mr. President, sometimes it's hard to lead young men and act courageous when all you really want to do is run and hide."

I felt as if Harry was going to speak up, so I interrupted him and cut him off, saying, "Yeah, I know. If you can't stand the heat, get out of the kitchen."

Sometimes, the right thing is easy to say and hard to do.

The next day, I was grading some papers in my U.S. History classroom when Bradley Hope came in.

He waited until I looked up at him and said, "Coach, can I talk to you for a minute?"

I told him it was my planning period, and then I had my lunch hour, so I motioned him to take a seat and join me.

I assured him, "Son, I have all the time we need. What's on your mind?"

Bradley cleared his throat and stated, "Coach, I need to know everything you understand about women."

I laughed until I almost cried, and when I could catch my breath, I responded, "Bradley, that won't take very long. I have found women to be a lot easier to enjoy than they are to understand. Of course, I'm sure they feel the same way about us."

Bradley nodded and explained, "When you first meet somebody, you don't quite know what to say or do, and you just don't want to do anything stupid or say the wrong thing."

I just nodded and beckoned for him to continue.

He sighed and said, "Then, when you get to know them a little better, it's hard to know what to tell them and how much they ought to know."

Suddenly, the enormity of what Bradley Hope was trying to share with me became clear.

I confirmed, "We're talking about Miss Gina, I assume."

Bradley nodded.

I stated truthfully, "She's a beautiful and talented young lady who obviously thinks a lot of you."

Bradley shrugged and mumbled, "I'm afraid if I tell her everything, she'll go away, and if I don't tell her, then everything between us isn't real."

I tried to reassure him. "I understand."

He asked, "Is it fair to ask somebody to go on a trip with you if you're not sure you're going to be there at the end…? And when do you tell them?"

I grasped for any shred of wisdom or bit of enlightenment I could bring to this situation.

I said, "You're probably not giving Gina enough credit in this situation. You and your mom are dealing with the reality of your diagnosis, and you seem to be holding up admirably. And when you told me, I didn't fall apart, so what makes you think Gina wouldn't be on your side?"

He thought for a minute and then replied, "Well, I don't have a choice in dealing with this, and neither does my mom."

He looked directly at me, and I could see tears forming in his eyes as he said, "And, Coach, you and I were sort of already connected when the cancer came along, so you're kind of stuck, too. But Gina doesn't really have to deal with this."

I nodded in understanding and posed what I hoped would be an insightful question because I felt I was out of answers.

I asked, "So, Bradley, if the positions were reversed, and you found out Gina had a serious problem, you probably wouldn't want to deal with it, and you might just run away and hide and let her handle it alone."

Bradley Hope slammed his open palm down on the desk top, causing a loud crack to reverberate throughout my classroom.

He shouted, "You know me better than that. I wouldn't do that to anybody."

I remained silent and hoped the logic of the situation would dawn on him. Slowly, a smile broke out across his face, and then I felt myself smiling.

"Son, I don't know Gina nearly as well as you do or as well as I hope to get to know her, but somehow I think when it comes to character, tenacity, and caring, she's probably a better person than you and me; so if we can stick together and face this thing, I think she's more than good enough to be on our team."

Chapter Eight

TEACHING AND LEARNING

*"Upon books the collective education
of the race depends; they are the sole
instruments of registering, perpetuating,
and transmitting thought."*
—HARRY S. TRUMAN

8

THE TEAM WAS IN A GREAT MOOD DURING PRACTICE THAT afternoon. Sometimes, the individual personalities fade away and become part of the collective attitude of the overall team. My Truman High Eagles were flying high after their first victory and looking forward to playing the Stonehill Jaguars that coming Friday.

Stonehill was a perennial rival of ours, but they were in what we coaches call a rebuilding year, and we were poised to exceed everyone's expectations if our first game performance was any indicator.

The players hung around the locker room after practice for a while, just being boys. Football takes a lot of focus, effort, and discipline. Additionally, these players had to concentrate on their studies and deal with many issues at home, so whenever possible, I thought it was good to let them blow off some steam as long as no one got hurt and it didn't get out of hand.

Finally, one by one and in small groups, they left the locker room, and I found myself alone in the coach's office. A deep despair had fallen over me that I couldn't shake, and I knew it was going to be a part of my life for a long time to come.

Bradley Hope's cancer hadn't just attacked him, but it had also attacked his mother, Gina, and me; and somehow I knew that the cancer in Bradley's body wasn't yet done attacking people's lives.

In hopes that President Harry S. Truman could provide some insight, I sat on a bench near his statue and waited for some wisdom to pour forth.

Harry had dealt with his share of depression and tragedy throughout his profound life. He had faced the end of World War II and the dropping of the atom bombs stoically, but it undoubtedly took a toll. Then he had to try to keep the Korean Conflict from escalating into World War III.

There were times when I'm certain he felt the weight of the world on his shoulders. During these times, I know that Harry found solace in listening to great music such as Chopin and Bach. He reveled in great poetry such as Tennyson's *Locksley Hall*, and he found escape as well as inspiration in great art from masters such as Frans Hals, Rubens, da Vinci, and Rembrandt. Rembrandt's *Descent from the Cross* was his favorite. That particular masterpiece has hung in the Hermitage since 1814.

During a time in my life when I couldn't spare the time or the money, I traveled to Russia to visit the Hermitage and see Rembrandt's *Descent from the Cross* for myself. I got to do and see many other things on that trip, but to be honest, I wanted to stand where Harry stood and try to experience what he felt. In some way, it created a unique bond between me and Harry. It seemed like we were connected through those magnificent brush strokes and shadows created by Rembrandt.

I think that the vulgarity of war hurt President Truman so much that he had to find solace in the beauty of music, art, and poetry.

When I was first exposed to poetry in Mrs. Drumright's World Literature class during my time as a student at Truman High, I snickered and rejected poetry as any good teenaged boy and football player thought that he was expected to do. Then, while skimming over one of Mrs. Drumright's homework assignments involving Rudyard Kipling's poem entitled *If*, I was captured. Kipling's words and phrases touched me in the deepest part of my soul. I couldn't believe that someone who lived and died before I was born could know my innermost thoughts and feelings so well.

I devoured each poem that was presented in Mrs. Drumright's class that year, and I became a lifelong, passionate fan of poetry.

Now that Mrs. Drumright was no longer my teacher but my colleague on the faculty whose classroom was situated across the hall from mine, we often took coffee breaks together or shared a brief moment in the hall to pass along our most recent poetic treasure discovery.

I continued to sit on the bench, waiting for Harry to provide some inspiration, but when none was immediately forthcoming, I decided to share some with him.

My grandfather often told me, "Sometimes, if you'll give away what you lack, you'll get what you need."

As a struggling college student, I found this to be true as I would often share my meager supply of food or financial resources with other students and then discover that my own needs were met shortly after.

Mrs. Drumright had recently given me a book of poetry entitled *Discovering Joye*. It was a compilation of poems written by Joye Kanelakos. Joye's poems were written throughout her life but were never shared until after her death. Joye was an average mother and housewife from a little town in the farmland. She wrote about her life, thoughts, and experiences and put them in a box that was discovered by her daughters after Joye Kanelakos's funeral.

Recently, those poems had been published and were beginning to impact people around the world. I thumbed through the little book that Eleanore Drumright had given me and found one I thought Harry might find to be uplifting.

I read,

> *"Surely, somewhere in my life*
> *There came a moment near sublime*
> *That we have shared, one fragile bliss—*
> *Remember this.*
> *"Or standing at a cavernous edge*
> *Where eons of stress had left its dredge*
> *Then draped it o'er in beautiful hue—*
> *Take this with you.*
> *"And should unhappiness try to stay*
> *Shut it aside. Recall that day*
> *We laughed 'til every hurt was gone—*
> *Please keep this one.*
> *"For anguish I have caused, forgive,*
> *And through life's unrelenting sieve*
> *Pluck out some shiny bit of me*
> *And kindly let all pain fall free—*
> *Do this for me."*

My grandfather was right. I couldn't be certain that Harry was inspired or found solace in Joye's poem, but I knew that I had.

I thought about Bradley Hope and a few rampaging cancer cells that had created crisis and turmoil for Bradley as well as so many others around him.

Throughout the rest of that week around the school, I seemed to run into Bradley and Gina everywhere. I guess it is kind of like when you buy a red car to be unique because you think no one else has one, and then it seems like all you pass on the road is one red car after another.

Bradley and Gina seemed to be good for one another. They laughed infectiously and then, obviously, had their serious, thoughtful moments.

Kids are more adaptable than adults. High school students are stuck in that proverbial "no-man's land" between being a child and being a grownup. As a coach and teacher, I saw high school kids at their best and worst. Sometimes, I was certain that I was dealing with a group of three-year-olds, and other times, they seemed more like thirty-three or forty-three.

Away games create a layer of complexity that does not exist when a team is playing a game at home. You have to make sure you have all of your right people in the right place at the right time with all of their equipment. I had great assistant coaches and equipment managers, but even so, for years I experienced lingering nightmares about lost players or missing equipment.

At the appointed hour on Friday afternoon, several school buses pulled up at the curb in the Harry S. Truman High School parking lot. These rickety, smoking buses would be our transportation to the Stonehill High stadium, 50 miles away.

The trip would take around an hour and a half; I knew from my many game-day trips to Stonehill as a player and coach. There were no superhighways or four-lane turnpikes. We would be bouncing along two-lane farm roads and passing through countless "one-horse" towns for an hour and a half.

Road trips put additional emotional demands on coaches and players. You can't go through your normal pre-game routine like you do for a home game because you have the team all together cooped up on the buses for the trip. On the other hand, you can't allow your team to get too emotionally high too early, or they will burn out long before the game begins, so I tried to keep it light and fun between me and the players as we were loading the buses and double-checking the equipment lists before departing.

Athletic coaches have become renowned for using their own clichés and unique language. Much of this language is coarse and foul among many coaches. This is something that I endeavored to avoid during my many years of coaching.

During my college days, I had read a book about the legendary basketball coach John Wooden. Coach Wooden won more national championships than anyone before or since. Sports fans argue whether or not there are any records that will never be broken. I go back and forth on this question, but if there is one record that will never be broken, I think it would have to involve Coach Wooden's national championships.

John Wooden had many elements of his life and career to recommend him, both as a coach and as a man. One of the many positive practices that I read Coach Wooden utilized through his years of coaching was the fact that he never used foul language. He often explained that we can't expect our young men to perform well under extreme pressure and control their emotions if we can't control our language.

My players gathered around me before boarding the buses. I looked at the expectant expressions on the young faces before me. I was expected to say something profound, but I didn't want to prematurely unleash the pregame emotion, so I told them about

Coach John Wooden and his policy on controlling your attitude and your language. I explained to my boys that I felt the same way, which was why they would only hear me using appropriate and uplifting language.

I told them, "Language is a tool that could be used to heal or hurt. Language has started wars and has ended wars. We are all susceptible to the language of others, but this is most true among our families and our teammates."

Just so I could leave the players with a bit of levity before the ordeal of the bus ride to Stonehill, I pointed to the statue of President Truman just beyond the huddled players and explained, "Now, President Truman had a bit of a challenge with language throughout his life. He loved to tell the story about his wife Bess being confronted by a matronly woman who was the head of a ladies' club where the president would be speaking. This woman apparently asked Bess if she could encourage the president to quit saying *manure*. Bess apparently told her that it had taken her 40 years to get the president to start saying *manure*.

The Truman High Eagles roared with laughter and climbed onto the various buses for the trip. I nodded to Harry and took my place in the first seat on the first bus of our convoy.

Mr. Stemseck was the principal at Harry S. Truman High during my playing days as well as much of my coaching and teaching career. He was always very positive about the football program and his belief that extracurricular activities were an important part of the educational process.

He was fond of saying, "A football field is a classroom with goalposts."

As the buses pulled away and the statue of Harry S. Truman faded into the distance, I reminded myself that most of these boys would never play football beyond their time with the Truman Eagles, but they would be husbands, fathers, businesspeople, and members of a community throughout their lives.

I spotted Bradley Hope seated across the aisle from me about six rows back and reminded myself that football games are not life and death.

Chapter Nine

LIFE AND DEATH

"It's a recession when your neighbor loses his job. It's a depression when you lose yours."
—HARRY S. TRUMAN

9

OUR BUSES RUMBLED AND BOUNCED UP AND DOWN HILLS AND around corners toward Stonehill. We passed through small towns, tiny burgs, and places too insignificant to have a name. I knew we were nearing Stonehill when the traffic picked up going toward the stadium, and we passed signs that had been placed along the road encouraging the Stonehill Jaguars to beat the Truman Eagles.

Cars filled with Stonehill students and fans passed our bus amidst shouts, honks, and waving signs. This was a time-tested ritual when approaching a town where we would be playing an away game. I had already instructed our players, coaches, and bus drivers to never respond to this.

As we turned onto the main street of Stonehill, a banner stretching from one side of the street to the other implored "Jaguars Ground the Eagles." The sidewalks were crowded with hometown people who pointed, yelled, and jeered at our buses and players.

Those who attended high school in big cities never experience this phenomenon. In a major metropolitan area, people don't even know that there's a game going on or who's playing, but in small-town America, it's like the Super Bowl.

Our driver pulled up to a gate in the fence that surrounded the Stonehill stadium. An attendant unlocked the gate, and our buses rolled through and stopped in front of the visitors' locker room.

My counterpart, Coach Ed Stockton, greeted me as I stepped down from the bus. Ed Stockton had been head coach of the Stonehill Jaguars for several years before I had gotten the head coaching job at Truman High School. Ed and I were not close friends, but we were cordial to one another while being intense competitors. He congratulated me on our win over Plainview, and I consoled him about his opening loss to Granite Ridge.

I said encouragingly, "Coach, they're a pretty tough team."

He laughed and responded, "I'm afraid they're all going to be pretty tough this year. We graduated a lot of good kids, and our cupboard is pretty bare."

We bantered back and forth for a few moments about the ups and downs of coaching until all of my players and assistant coaches had made their way into the visitors' locker room.

I thanked Coach Stockton for being on hand to greet us.

He nodded and replied half-jokingly, "Well, Coach Fullerton, I want to wish you good luck on this whole football season except for tonight."

We both laughed heartily, shook hands, and parted company. I went into the locker room to be with my team, and Coach Stockton headed across the field to go through his own pregame routine with his kids.

Visiting locker rooms never seem big enough. In your own stadium, there's a place for everything, and everything is in its place. Our boys finally sorted out all of their gear, donned their visiting uniforms, and seemed to be ready to get down to business. I got their attention and began.

"Gentlemen, this will not be like last week when we had our own people in our own stadium. Everyone out there came here tonight to see you get beat. We need to jump on these people quick and get a lead in order to take the crowd out of the game. If you let a team like this hang around too long, the momentum can really overwhelm you."

They all nodded in understanding, and I ended by saying, "Guys, it's still a game, and we're still here to have fun, so let's get after it."

As the voice of the stadium announcer declared, "And let's welcome our visitors, the Truman High Eagles," we were met with a chorus of boos and catcalls. Road trips seem to draw teams together. It invokes that sort of "It's us against the world" feeling.

Our offense had performed so well the previous week, and I was starting to think that the sky was the limit with our quarterback, Jessie Hunter, so when we won the coin toss, we chose to receive the kickoff.

Harry himself said, "Carry the battle to them. Don't let them bring it to you. Put them on the defensive, and don't ever apologize for anything."

I felt like if we could jump out to an early lead, we could get Stonehill out of the game both mentally and physically. That's just the way it happened.

The Eagles drove the ball 80 yards down the field in nine plays, and we scored on an eight-yard pass to our tight end in the corner of the end zone. Hunter put the ball right where it needed to be.

Great quarterbacks can throw a pass in such a way that their receiver can catch it, but it's completely out of the reach of any defenders. A pass like that one either results in a touchdown or the ball going harmlessly out of bounds.

Our kicker put the extra point through the uprights, and we had a seven-to-nothing lead just a few minutes into the contest.

Stonehill fumbled our kickoff at the 12-yard-line, and they were forced to fall on the loose ball and begin their first drive deep in their own territory. Our defense seemed eager to build upon the success of the offense's first scoring drive, so we stopped Stonehill in three straight plays, forcing them to punt.

Their punter got a lot of distance out of his kick but very little height. Hang time is a critical element of football. It measures the number of seconds between the punter's foot striking the ball and the receiving team's player catching it. If the ball is kicked too far and too low, the kicking team's players cannot get down the field to cover the punt, therefore allowing the receiving team to get a great return.

Rarely do plays unfold the way you draw them up on the board, but every once in a while, it all comes together. Our man fielded the punt cleanly and headed for the left sideline, just as we had planned. The other ten Eagles got good, clean blocks on the Jaguars, and our punt returner raced into the end zone without even being touched.

I made a mental note to pay special attention to that punt return when we were reviewing the game films. I knew I would enjoy watching it unfold again. It would end up in my highlight reel that I would share with Truman Eagles for years to come. That kind of moment lives in the hearts and minds of players for the rest of their lives.

Another extra point followed, and we were up 14 to nothing. The Stonehill Jaguars' crowd quieted, and their players seemed to move a little slower with their heads hanging down dejectedly.

I didn't want to take my foot off the gas too quickly, but I didn't want to let the game get too lopsided because we would be playing against Coach Stockton again next year and for many years to come. It was only a matter of time until he had a great team, and we would be in a rebuilding year with our own bare cupboards.

The game rolled on, and by the fourth quarter we were ahead 42 to 14. A lot of backup players had gotten to play some meaningful minutes, and the only Eagle who hadn't gotten into the game was Bradley Hope. He was standing next to me, and I was describing that I wanted him to go in for the next play, but it never happened.

Although the Stonehill Jaguars had no chance of winning the game, they continued to play hard and compete. This was a good testament to the positive influence of Coach Ed Stockton.

Their quarterback dropped back to pass and fired the ball over the middle toward his receiver. The pass was high, but the Jaguar split end leapt high in the air. Just as his outstretched fingers grazed the football, our defensive safety rushed in to deliver a jarring hit. The ball fell to the grass harmlessly, and the Jaguar receiver was upended and crashed to the field. A collective gasp was heard throughout the stadium, and then everyone fell silent.

Football can be a violent game, but for the most part, players only inflict bumps and bruises upon one another; however, I knew to the depth of my being that this was different.

It had been a clean and legal hit. Our safety, Cliff Nolan, had done nothing wrong. He had played the game the way it was meant to be played. I was glad for him that he had not been involved in an illegal hit or a cheap shot because I was certain this would be more than a bump or a bruise.

Their receiver lay on the turf, motionless. I rushed toward him from our side of the field just as Coach Stockton raced to the aid of his downed player from his own sideline. The other players backed away and took a knee. Some prayed silently, and others just looked off into space.

Bradley Hope joined the players on the field as he had already raced out to take the place of one of our defensive players. He never did get into that game, but that was the least of our worries.

As I was preparing to kneel down next to the injured Jaguar, I felt a hand on my back, and the familiar voice of Dr. Ryan calmly said, "Let me get in there, Coach. I think this is more my line than yours right now."

In more than four decades of playing and coaching football, I have seen a lot of injured players, but this was different. The young man was completely motionless. I suspected he had been knocked unconscious. I was just hoping and praying that he would wake up and be able to move his arms and legs.

The Stonehill team had an athletic trainer who was, no doubt, an expert at taping ankles and dealing with turf burns, but he was more than happy to yield to Dr. Ryan in this situation.

After what seemed like an eternity but was probably only a minute or two, Steve Ryan turned to me with a cool, expressionless demeanor and stated, "Coach, we're going to need the ambulance."

I signaled to the ambulance in the end zone frantically, and the attendant drove onto the field and stopped beside the injured player.

Dr. Ryan gave the ambulance attendants some very specific instructions, and they carefully got the player onto a stretcher and into the ambulance.

I patted Ed Stockton on the back, and he jumped into the back of the ambulance with his fallen player.

I called, "Hang in there, Ed. All of our prayers will go with you."

Ed looked directly into my eyes and nodded his thanks as Dr. Ryan jumped into the ambulance and knelt beside the player. They closed the ambulance door and drove away.

My heart sank as I realized that the nearest regional hospital was the one outside of Springfield where Dr. Ryan practiced. It had taken us an hour and a half to get here, but I knew the ambulance could make it in half that time.

The referee had just finished talking with the Stonehill assistant coach and approached me, saying, "Coach, less than 30 seconds left on the clock. Can we all agree to just let the time run off?"

I nodded and motioned for our assistant coaches and players to head for the locker room. I shook hands with their assistant and told him we would all be pulling for the young man.

I asked, "Coach, what's the boy's name?"

He replied solemnly, "Steve Gaylord... He's a good kid."

I nodded and headed for the locker room.

It was a somber atmosphere in the visitors' locker room under Stonehill Stadium that night. To an outside observer, it would have seemed more like we lost the game instead of winning it handily. I got all the players' attention and told them they'd played well. I told them the injured player was named Steve Gaylord. We came together for a brief word of prayer.

I tried to encourage as many of the boys as I could as they were getting dressed and packing their gear. I made it a special point to find Cliff Nolan, and I sat on the bench next to him.

I stated emphatically, "Son, you played a good game including the hit on their receiver. It could have happened to anyone."

He nodded silently in understanding, but I noticed a tear at the corner of his eye. In some ways, his future was hanging in the balance like Steve Gaylord's. They were two young men who had never met and hadn't even known one another's names, but now they were linked together by a macabre bond.

As I headed for the locker room door to get on the bus, I spotted Bradley Hope in front of me.

I patted his shoulder and said, "Hope, I'm sorry we couldn't get you in the game, but..."

Bradley Hope turned to me and said the words that will remain in my heart and soul until the day I die.

"Coach, I understand the difference between a game and life and death."

Chapter Ten

BALANCE AND PERSPECTIVE

"When even one American who has done nothing wrong is forced by fear to shut his mind and close his mouth, then all Americans are in peril."
—HARRY S. TRUMAN

10

I RAN ACROSS THE PARKING LOT AND INTO THE MAIN ENTRANCE OF Springfield Regional Hospital. The automatic doors slid open for me and closed behind me.

I rushed up to an information desk and breathlessly inquired, "Steve Gaylord?"

The young woman at the hospital desk nodded and consulted a computer screen then turned, picked up a phone, and spoke quietly to someone for a brief minute.

She turned back to me with a somber look on her face and said, "Sir, he's still in the emergency room, and they're prepping him for surgery."

I just stood there in stunned silence, and she continued, "Are you a relative?"

"Well, not exactly," I muttered. I took a deep breath and explained, "Ma'am, I'm a football coach, and this is really important, and the boy was injured in a game..."

She nodded in understanding and stated officially, "Coach, I understand your situation. My father was a football coach for many years, but I have to mark this form, and the fact of the matter is, if you're a relative you go down the hall to the left and wait with the rest of the family in the emergency room waiting area. And if you're not a relative, you have to wait out here in the lobby."

I nodded my understanding, got a brief flash of inspiration, and declared, "Ma'am, I've always told my boys that we are a family. We play together, stick together, win together, and even lose together, so to answer your question, I'm family."

She smiled broadly, marked her form, and said politely, "Well, the waiting room is down the hall to the left, and it will mean a lot to everyone to have Steve's uncle there with them."

"Your father would be proud of you," I said over my shoulder as I rushed toward the emergency room waiting area.

Coach Ed Stockton was sitting alone in the middle of a long row of chairs. He was fidgeting nervously and trying to read a magazine. He noticed me approaching, and I could tell he was both surprised and pleased to have me there.

I inquired, "Coach, how's our boy?"

Ed shook his head slowly and replied, "He's still unconscious. We don't know anything yet. We're just waiting to hear."

As he seemed to be totally alone, I didn't understand his use of the word "we," and I asked, "Does he have family, and are they on the way?"

Coach Stockton sighed in frustration and explained, "His father's over there in that corner." Then he turned 180 degrees and continued, "And his mother is in the opposite corner. They are separated."

"Obviously so," I observed.

I sat down with Coach Stockton, and we tried to make small talk and carry on some football dialogue to avoid the one topic that was dominating both of our minds.

Eventually, Dr. Steve Ryan emerged from a metal door at the far end of the waiting room and approached us.

He said, "Coach Stockton and Coach Fullerton, I wanted to give everyone an update."

Dr. Ryan gazed around the room and continued, "Is the family here?"

Coach Stockton explained, "Yes and no." He pointed at the two parents in opposite corners of the room and continued, "If you can fill me in, I'll do my best to keep everybody up to speed."

Steve Ryan shrugged and explained, "He's still unconscious with no muscle reaction at all. We've got a ventilator breathing for him, and I've called for a neurosurgeon who should be arriving shortly on a helicopter from the state capital. I'll let you know when there's any more information."

Dr. Ryan turned on his heels and rushed back through the metal door to the emergency room. Coach Stockton began pacing back and forth, and I decided to go for a walk and give him some space.

I mumbled, "Ed, I'm going to get a little air."

He just mumbled something and nodded.

As I walked along the hall, I spotted a sign that indicated the cafeteria was to the right, the maternity ward was straight ahead, and the chapel was to my left. Without thinking about it, I turned to the left and made my way along the corridor. I peeked in the door of the chapel and noticed a nun sitting there alone, quietly praying.

I backed away so as not to disturb her, but I heard her call out to me, "Please come in."

She met me inside the chapel door, held her hand out to me, and introduced herself. "I am Sister Mary Florene."

I shook her hand and said, "Sister, I am Coach Glen Fullerton."

She nodded knowingly and beckoned me to sit down. I joined her on the padded bench, and she inquired, "So, Coach Fullerton, what brings you here tonight?"

I explained to her that my team had been in Stonehill for a football game, and on the last play, one of their players was injured.

She asked, "So, it wasn't one of your players?"

I shook my head and replied, "Sister, before the injury, it was a football game—us against them—but after that play, it felt like we were all on the same team."

She nodded and said, "I like that, but I'll admit to not knowing a lot about football."

I replied awkwardly, "Well, Sister, I'll admit to not knowing a lot about…your line of work."

She beckoned, "Well, why don't you tell me what you do as a football coach."

I explained how I try to help young boys become young men and teach them lessons that they can carry with them throughout their lives.

Sister Mary Florene chuckled softly. I turned to her, and she said, "Forgive me, but it seems that you and I are in much the same line of work."

She offered a brief but earnest prayer for Steve Gaylord and walked with me back to the emergency room waiting area. We arrived just as the emergency room door banged open, and Dr. Ryan rushed over to us.

He said, "Well, he's stable for the moment. I do have a brief update for the parents."

Sister Mary Florene asked, "Where is the family?"

Coach Stockton explained, "Well, Sister, the mother and father are separated and apparently not willing to speak to one another or hardly even be in the same room."

Sister Mary Florene glanced toward the far corner and saw the mother sitting there. Then she turned so she could see the father in the opposite corner.

She announced, rather forcefully, "That is totally unacceptable."

Then she turned, took a few steps toward the mother, and called, "Mrs. Gaylord? You will come over here and join us right now."

Then she turned toward the father and called, "Mr. Gaylord, you will walk over here and stand next to your wife right this minute."

Coach Stockton and I both were in awe as the parents dutifully rushed over and stood next to one another.

Sister Mary Florene nodded and declared, "Now, that's better." She turned to Dr. Ryan and prompted, "Doctor, I believe you have a report for us."

Steve Ryan explained, "Well, he's out of any immediate danger, and he's awake and alert, but right now has no movement below the neck."

His mother gasped and began to cry.

Dr. Ryan continued, "We don't know whether that's a permanent condition or not. The neurosurgeon from the state capital is here, and he's going to try to take some pressure off the spinal cord, and then we just have to wait and see."

Mrs. Gaylord continued to cry softly, and her husband actually put his arm around her to comfort her.

Dr. Ryan tried to reassure them, saying, "Folks, this surgeon is the best there is."

I briefly introduced myself to Steve Gaylord's mother and father, then told Ed Stockton I would check in with him a little later.

Sister Mary Florene gave everyone an encouraging word and then turned to me. "Coach Fullerton, I'll walk out with you."

Once we were out of earshot of the emergency room waiting area, I turned to her and said, "Sister, that was quite an impressive performance."

She laughed playfully and said in a soft voice with no hint of the power she had displayed earlier, "Sometimes we just have to do whatever it takes to bring people together."

I laughed and offered, "Well, Sister, if you ever decide you'd like to be on my staff as an assistant football coach, you've got a job."

She laughed with me and said, "I may be calling you someday."

"Any time," I stated, "but you would have to learn how to work under a head coach while you're doing your job."

Sister Mary Florene fingered the cross around her neck and replied, "I believe I have acquired the knack of working under the supervision of a head coach."

I nodded in understanding and thought how different our two worlds were but, on another level, how much they were alike.

I remembered Harry's statement, "Believing is halfway there."

I glanced at Sister Mary Florene and held on to that thought.

Throughout that week, my team prepared for our upcoming game with the Baytown Bobcats. Playing Baytown was an unusual game for us in that they are a top division school that is in a conference with the elite teams across the state.

Old Coach Bartlett always said, "You don't get any better beating up on a weakling or even competing against someone at your own level."

He had always scheduled at least one game a year with one of the top-ranked, larger schools. This is a practice I had continued, and that's how we came to be playing Baytown that coming Friday.

In keeping with my policy and commitment to my team, I repeatedly told them throughout the week, "They are bigger, faster, and more talented than we are at most positions. If they play their very best, they should beat us, but never forget, that if we play our very best game of the year and they let down, we could actually beat these people."

Football is an unpredictable game, played with an unpredictable ball. A baseball or basketball are round and bounce the same way in a predictable fashion every time. A football is like life. You never know which way the ball is going to bounce at any second, so you've got to be ready for anything.

I stayed in contact with Dr. Ryan and Ed Stockton each day, and by the end of that week, Steve Gaylord was out of danger but still paralyzed. Only time would tell which way the football would bounce for him.

The night before the Baytown game, I stopped off on my way out of the school building to give President Truman an update. I told him there was nothing new regarding Steve Gaylord's medical situation, and I shared with him my anxiety about being a real underdog in the upcoming game.

Harry Truman had a dream to go to West Point as a young man, but his poor eyesight kept him out of the academy. He had many political liabilities in his career, but overcame all the odds to occupy the White House.

He was fond of saying, "You know that being an American is more than a matter of where your parents came from. It is a belief that all men are created free and equal and that everyone deserves an even break."

I said goodnight to Harry, and as I walked away I thought, *I hope Truman's words come true for the Truman Eagles tomorrow night.*

Chapter Eleven

BEST AND BETTER

"If you can't convince them, confuse them."
—HARRY S. TRUMAN

11

BAYTOWN WAS EVERYTHING SPRINGFIELD WASN'T. IT WAS AN UPSCALE suburb on the edge of our state's largest metropolitan area. The Baytown Bobcats' football team was also everything we weren't. I had watched them constantly on game film throughout the week trying to find the illusive Eagle's Edge.

Being a history teacher myself, I've long thought that history is a lot like watching a game film. Often, you can learn things from the past that will help you in the future. There was no way we could line up head to head and play against Baytown, so I began to work some gadget or trick plays into our game plan.

Being a part of the largest city in the state, Baytown football is covered daily in several major newspapers. One of the reporters, named Joe Schneider, had written an article each day leading up to the game. He described how the Baytown Bobcats were invincible, and the Truman Eagles simply didn't have a chance. I clipped out every one of his offerings and displayed them on the bulletin board in our locker room.

Joe Schneider called me for a comment a couple of days before the game. He laughed and asked, "Coach, do you really think you're good enough?"

I responded, "It depends on what you mean by *good enough*."

I went on to tell him an often-repeated story about President Truman. Apparently, Harry was on one of his routine daily walks that he called *constitutionals*. In the middle of his brisk walk, the president confronted a homeless man sitting on the curb beside a trash can, drinking from a bottle of liquor.

The president greeted him and asked, "How is it?"

The homeless man responded, "Good enough."

The president inquired, "What do you mean?"

The homeless man took another drink and answered, "Well, the man that owns this house threw this bottle in the trash can. If it had been any better, he wouldn't have thrown it out; and if it had been any worse, I wouldn't drink it. So I guess it's good enough."

I hung up on Joe Schneider, leaving him to figure out the point of the story.

Mr. Schneider always put me in mind of a famous Truman quote. "It is ignorance that causes most mistakes."

Harry Truman had been fond of playing poker. He always felt that his skills in bluffing helped him at the end of World War II.

Harry became president after the death of Franklin Roosevelt. Shortly after being sworn in, Secretary of War Henry Stimson, with other officials, came into the oval office and informed President Truman that we had developed the atomic bomb, and it could be instrumental in ending the war.

Realizing that the atomic bomb could actually save lives by avoiding a ground war in Japan, the Truman Administration called for the Japanese to surrender then ordered the first bomb to be dropped. Hiroshima was utterly devastated. The Truman Administration again called on Japan to surrender; however, the Japanese would not comply, so the order was given for the second bomb to be dropped. Nagasaki was destroyed, and it was announced that we would continue dropping bombs until the Japanese unconditionally surrendered, which they did. What was not fully understood at the time was the fact that we had only developed a limited number of atomic bombs, and it would have been very costly, both in budgetary and in political terms, for the administration to continue dropping atomic bombs on Japan; but Harry's plan had worked, and the war was over. His residual poker skills involving bluffing had been a significant factor in ending World War II.

As I stood looking up at the statue of Harry one day after practice, I told him about our new camouflage player strategy, the flea-flicker, and our hidden ball trick. Somehow, I felt he would be pleased.

On game day, I left the school early and headed across the parking lot to our stadium.

While the statue of Harry Truman is an ever-present fixture in front of the school, as one enters the Truman Eagles football stadium they pass a statue of Emma Quinn. Miss Quinn—never Mrs. or Ms. Quinn—had been a teacher at Truman High School for her entire adult life. I struggled through her geometry and statistics classes myself and then served on the faculty with her for two years until she retired.

The reason Miss Quinn's statue adorns our stadium is one of the truly great American success stories. Apparently, Emma Quinn was a diligent saver and investor throughout her life. When Old Coach Bartlett called an emergency meeting of the school board after the rickety wooden bleachers had been partially destroyed in a fire set by some vandals, Coach Bartlett pounded the table and demanded that Truman High build a modern football stadium.

The head of the school board informed the coach that was out of the question and could not even be considered as a budget item for many years into the future.

A loud argument ensued and continued until Miss Quinn slowly walked up to the podium and got everyone's attention.

She announced, "Mr. Chairman, school board members, faculty, and staff. I'm a math teacher and believe that academics are the most important function of a school."

Coach Bartlett rose to object, but Miss Quinn continued. "But, on the other hand, extracurricular activities play an important role in young people's development, and this football stadium could be a point of pride for not only our school but the entire community."

The school board chairman rose to reiterate the budget problems, but Miss Quinn motioned for silence and pressed on. "So, to that end, I would like to make a donation myself to the new Harry S. Truman High Eagles Football Stadium."

An awkward silence fell over the room, and a few incredulous chuckles could be heard as the chairman spoke. "Miss Quinn, while we all appreciate your expertise as a teacher as well as your offer to make a donation, a modern stadium would cost over a million dollars."

Miss Quinn nodded and corrected him. "Sir, it would actually cost $1.82 million, to be precise, and I always endeavor to be precise."

The chairman objected, "But, ma'am, we don't have the wherewithal to raise that money."

Miss Quinn assumed her teaching pose and observed, "Sir, you're obviously not listening. I just told you I am going to make a donation."

One of the board members said, in frustration, "This is a waste of time. What good could a few hundred or even a few thousand dollars do toward this stadium?"

Miss Quinn shook her head disappointedly and spoke as if addressing a failing student. "You, sir, are also not listening. I am not going to donate a few hundred or even a few thousand dollars."

He objected, "Miss Quinn, just how much do you expect to donate?"

"If you were in my statistics class, I would have to give you poor marks for paying attention." She stared at everyone until the room fell silent again, then continued. "I am prepared to donate the sum of $1.82 million for the stadium."

As I looked up at the statue of that little woman, I thought about how small beginnings sometimes could end with big results. I hoped something like that might happen that very night as we played the Baytown Bobcats.

As I stood on the sideline and watched our team warming up, I periodically glanced down to the other end of the stadium and watched Baytown going through their pregame drills. They looked huge.

When one of my assistant coaches sidled up next to me and exclaimed, "Wow, those guys are big," I tried to contain the panic and quipped, "No, it's just the light blue uniforms make them appear larger than they are."

My assistant looked at me with a confused expression on his face.

I explained, "It's a fashion concept my Aunt Madge told me about when I was a kid."

He walked away with a bewildered expression on his face, but when I ambled down to the far end of the stadium to greet their head coach, I couldn't help noticing that the Baytown Bobcats were, indeed, huge whatever color of uniforms they might be wearing.

I inquired, "Coach Rydell?"

He stuck out his hand and answered, "Yes, and you must be…" The man actually had to check the sheet on his clipboard before he continued. "…Coach Fullerton."

I nodded.

He proclaimed, "Well, it doesn't seem like much of a matchup. I hope your boys can give us a decent game."

I fought down the anger rising up inside of me and replied, "It'll be a game."

I turned and walked away without further comment.

We kicked off to Baytown, and they drove right down the field and scored as if we weren't there. Our boys were playing hard and got into position, but they just couldn't stop the bigger, faster opponents.

But then we scored on our first possession with our flawlessly executed flea-flicker play. Our quarterback pitched the ball to our halfback, who seemed to be racing around the left end until he stopped, reared back, and threw the football into the end zone where our tight end was standing unnoticed.

The Truman High fans went wild, and the first quarter ended with the score tied 7 to 7.

Baytown scored two more touchdowns in the first half, but our camouflage player trick play paid off.

After I had called a time out, I sent 10 players out into the huddle. They milled around so the Bobcats wouldn't notice we were a man short. Meanwhile, all of our players along the sideline moved right up to the edge of the field, and just before the ball was snapped, one of them stepped across the out-of-bounds line and became an instant unseen split end. He just looked like one of the other players standing along the sideline.

Before the Bobcats knew what hit them, he raced down the sideline and caught a perfect pass from our quarterback, Jessie Hunter, making the halftime score 21 to 14.

In the halftime locker room, our players seemed excited and hopeful even though we were one touchdown behind. The assistant coaches gave the position players their various responsibilities for the second half, and I got everyone's attention to give them a final word before we took the field.

"Gentlemen, if nothing else, our success in the first half clearly proves we can play with these people. They are sitting over there in the visitors' locker room on the other side of the stadium trying to figure out what happened to them. We have a tremendous advantage because we know what it's like to work hard and struggle, and the Baytown Bobcats have never been in a tough game...until tonight."

The Eagles cheered, shouted, and roared as they rushed onto the field for the second half.

Bradley Hope was like a tornado on the sideline that second half. He cheered, yelled, and met every player coming off the field. I was really proud of him that night. Reserve players that usually ride the bench know that there is absolutely no way they are going to get into a tight game with a top-flight opponent, but if Bradley wasn't going to get onto the field, he was at least going to do everything he could to make sure that the boys who did get on the field gave it their best.

His actions and attitude reminded me of one of my favorite quotes from Harry. "All the president is, is a glorified public relations man who spends his time flattering, kissing, and kicking people to get them to do what they are supposed to do anyway."

If Bradley Hope could fulfill President Truman's definition of a glorified public relations man, I thought that the least I could do in the second half of that struggle with the Baytown Bobcats was to be the leader of the Truman Eagles. On every play, regardless of the outcome, I forced myself to exude a calm confidence as if I knew we deserved to be on the field with this team, and we were going to compete to the end.

It reminded me of another of Harry's famous quotes. "Men make history and not the other way around. In periods where there is no leadership, society stands still. Progress occurs when courageous, skillful leaders seize the opportunity to change things for the better."

We stayed in that game with nothing more than smoke and mirrors. I was never more proud of my team than that night. It came down to a last-second field goal, and they beat us 24 to 21. Baytown had won, but the Truman High School Eagles were victorious.

I walked across the field to congratulate Coach Rydell on the win.

He shook my hand heartily and sincerely stated, "Coach Fullerton, I believe that was the finest performance by an opposing team I've ever seen."

I expressed my thanks and began to move away.

He stopped me saying, "Coach, I'm wondering if you would allow me the privilege of doing something a bit unusual."

I nodded for him to continue.

He stated, "I'd like to say a word to your boys."

Coach Rydell was right about one thing. His request was a bit unusual. In fact, in over 40 years of coaching, that was the only time it happened.

I went into the locker room, encouraged my players who were all a bit dejected, but I told them to hold their heads up high, and I announced, "Gentlemen, we have a guest who would like to say a word to you."

I walked to the locker room door and shoved it open. Coach Rydell walked in. My team wouldn't have been any more surprised if they had gotten a visit from the Queen of England, but I was proud of them. They were polite and respectful to Coach Rydell.

He cleared his throat and spoke. "First, I want to thank your coach, Glen Fullerton, for allowing me to say a few words to you. You're lucky to have a man like him leading you. I have to admit I was outcoached tonight by quite a lot."

Coach Rydell looked at me and gave a nod of respect then continued, "Men, we have better players, but you are a better team. You should have lost that game by four or five touchdowns, but we had to hit a last-second field goal to pull it out. You should be proud of your performance, proud of your team, and proud of yourselves."

Coach Rydell shook my hand and walked out of our locker room. There was nothing else to be said.

Chapter Twelve

SIGHT AND VISION

"America was not built on fear. America was built on courage, on imagination, and an unbeatable determination to do the job at hand."
—HARRY S. TRUMAN

12

OVER THE NEXT FEW WEEKS, WE BEAT RIVERSIDE 28 TO 24, Gainesville 21 to 17, and Chatsworth 31 to 21. All the games were relatively close, so many of our reserve players, including Bradley Hope, didn't get to play.

Even though he hadn't gotten into a game yet, Bradley Hope was making an amazing contribution to our team that year. His spirit and enthusiasm lifted everyone, and he was a positive force during practice on our scout team.

Scout teams have a difficult and thankless job. They review game film of the upcoming opponent and try to emulate that opponent so that our starting team can practice against the opponent's plays and formations. Bradley took it seriously and made each play count. It was like he was competing in the Super Bowl.

As I reviewed our record thus far in that season and looked at the schedule of games still to come, it became obvious that if we could win the next game we would make it into the playoffs. That was easier said than done, as we would be playing the Granite Ridge Giants the next Friday.

Granite Ridge had been Truman High's arch rival throughout my playing days and my coaching career. Some teams just create a more competitive atmosphere and a desire to win. Granite Ridge always did that for us. As a player and a coach, you want to win every game, but if you can beat your fiercest rival, the victory is extra sweet.

I was sitting in my office that Wednesday before the Granite Ridge game working on my athletic department budgets. There are few things I hate worse than dealing with paperwork, receipts, and school board forms. People who complain about the waste of their tax dollars may be justified on some fronts but not at Harry S. Truman High School. Not only did teachers and coaches never waste a penny, most of them provided supplies that they paid for out of their own pockets.

President Truman himself became legendary for being stingy with federal tax dollars as well as blunt and forthright in his written correspondence. As president, he had unlimited franking privileges allowing him to mail personal or professional letters free of charge through the White House service; however, Harry was dogged in his rejection of using this privilege for his personal mail when he wanted to express himself in writing in a manner he knew his staff would want to clean up.

Harry's daughter, Margaret, was an aspiring opera singer, and due to her famous father, she got booked to sing in concert halls that may have been made possible more by her last name than her talent; therefore, Margaret received many scathing reviews of her singing in newspapers across the country.

Harry took it upon himself to write several of those critics a personal letter condemning their criticism of his daughter. After sealing each of those letters himself, he stubbornly reached into his own wallet and took out a three-cent stamp, affixing it to the envelope which he then gave to one of the staff messengers with the instructions to deposit the letter in a public mailbox on the street. This insured that the music critic would receive Harry's thoughts without having his words censored by White House personnel.

I was thinking about Harry's frugality and sense of honor when my budget struggles were mercifully interrupted by a knock on the door. If I had been given a hundred guesses as to who had been calling on me that day, I would not have guessed that Ray Cline, the head coach of the Granite Ridge Giants, had come to see me.

Coach Cline and I had been very competitive rivals for a number of years. Some coaches from opposing teams manage to generate a sense of camaraderie and even casual friendship, but Coach Cline and I had never approached those elements in our relationship.

I called, "Come in," and Coach Cline opened my office door and stepped in.

The shock must have registered on my face, and Coach Cline declared, "I bet you're surprised to see me."

I nodded and replied, "I didn't expect to see you until we shook hands at midfield at the game Friday night."

He nodded, and I motioned for him to sit down. After we both settled into an awkward silence, I determined to let him speak first.

Finally, he leaned back into his chair, blew out a long breath, and began. "Coach Fullerton, I know it's a bit strange for me to be calling on you the week of our game, but I've got a bit of a situation that's going to unfold Friday night, and I thought I ought to share it with you."

My curiosity was piqued, and I nodded for him to continue.

He explained, "Coach, I have a young man who played on my team for the last two years. He's a good kid and had some potential as a ballplayer; but then last summer, he took a job in a manufacturing plant in our town and was blinded in a freak industrial accident."

I remembered the incident and said, "Yes, I read about that in the newspaper and thought about what a great tragedy that was."

I had, indeed, thought about that young man quite a bit since learning about his accident, particularly after I became aware of Bradley Hope's situation. When you dedicate your life to teaching and coaching high school kids, you don't expect to deal with death and disability.

I still didn't understand why that sad incident last summer had prompted a visit from Coach Cline that day.

I inquired, "So, Coach, how can I help you today?"

He stated, "The fact of the matter is, that boy is gonna play in our game Friday night."

I was elated and exclaimed, "That's great! I guess the doctors were able to help him."

Ray Cline shook his head sadly and replied, "No, he's still totally blind."

I was baffled and asked, "But he's going to play in our game Friday night?"

Coach Ray Cline nodded his head emphatically and said, "Donnie Amos went to a rehabilitation center for a while to learn how to live as a blind person, and while he was there, the kid taught himself to be a kicker."

He apparently saw the shock on my face and continued, "No, really, Coach. He showed up at my practice on Monday and showed me what he could do. Once he lines up the direction in his mind, he's like any other kicker. The snapper delivers the ball to the holder who gets it on the tee, and Donnie kicks it. He asked to get back on the team, and I could tell it was really important to him."

I nodded and said, "Well, I guess you'd have to let him back on the team right there on the spot."

My respect for Coach Ray Cline grew immensely as he shook his head and stated, "No way was I going to let him back on my team just because he was blind and wanted to be a Granite Ridge Giant again."

I was beginning to understand and asked, "So what did you do?"

He said, "I set up a tryout for him after practice, and he competed head-to-head against our regular kicker. It was close, but Donnie actually had better distance and more accuracy than our regular guy."

"Wow," I exclaimed. "That's great, but..."

I held out my hands, palms up, trying to express my ongoing confusion about the visit.

He explained, "Coach Fullerton, the reason I'm here today is there's been a lot of media inquiries about this thing. You know, having a blind kicker and all, and it's probably all going to hit the fan on Friday night."

I nodded in understanding and thanked Coach Cline for coming in to tell me about it. I walked him to the door and all the way out of the building to his car in the parking lot. I felt a real respect growing between us and the possible hint of a budding friendship.

He shook my hand, got into his car, and drove away. I walked back toward my office but stopped to share a moment with Harry.

I looked up at that wise countenance recreated by a sculptor and said, "Well, Harry, I know you wanted to get into West Point and were rejected because your eyesight was so poor; but then you became a successful officer and hero during World War I, commanding Company D. When it was all said and done, you may have accomplished more for the war effort than the guys who got into the military academy."

As I walked away, President Truman's own words rang in my head, heart, and soul. "The reward of suffering is experience."

There was always a huge crowd in the stands and a lot of excitement any time Truman High played Granite Ridge. But that Friday night, it seemed like there was more energy and enthusiasm than ever before, and as Coach Cline had guessed, there was a lot of media covering the game and, particularly, Donnie Amos's resurrection as a player for Granite Ridge. Not only were there the standard local newspaper reporters and radio announcers, there were television cameras on the sidelines representing some national networks.

I tried to prepare my team in the locker room with my pregame speech.

"Gentlemen, you know what it means for Truman to beat Granite Ridge, and you know what it means when we have to live with it all year when they beat us. It's really not a successful season, no matter what else we do, if we don't beat them, and I know they feel the same way about us. Well, it's no secret that there's a lot of media coverage out there because their blind kicker will be playing his first game tonight."

I paused and looked at my team arranged around me in the locker room, and then I continued, "I know you will handle this situation and the media with great respect, and I know you will treat their kicker like you would want someone to treat one of your teammates if the roles were reversed."

One of our captains, an outstanding defensive end, stood and spoke. "Coach, no problem. Some of us have talked about it, and we'll take it easy on him and won't block his kick or anything."

With a ferocity I would not have imagined, Bradley Hope leapt to his feet and shouted, "No way!"

Every eye in the locker room was riveted on Hope as he explained, "Each one of us made this team because we worked harder and were better than somebody who didn't make the team. That's why it means something to have this jersey."

Hope grasped his Truman Eagles jersey and continued, "This blind kid playing for them is no different. In fact, more than any of us, he needs to know that he is legitimate and that he deserves to be on the field, just like anyone else."

Hope aimed his stare directly at the defensive end who had spoken earlier. Hope was half his size but challenged him.

"If you can block that kid's kick, you do it. He deserves your best effort, just like the rest of us do."

That formidable defensive end nodded his head in understanding and respect, looked at Bradley Hope, and said, "Thanks, Hope."

It was a tough game like any Granite Ridge and Truman contest. The momentum swung back and forth, and there was the heightened energy of the huge crowd and the media coverage. We held a touchdown lead into the fourth quarter when Granite Ridge scored and was an extra point away from tying the game.

A hush fell over the stadium as one of the Granite Ridge players led Donnie Amos onto the field to kick the extra point. I had already watched him perform several times at earlier points in the game when he had kicked extra points and an impressive 38-yard field goal. I couldn't help but feel great for his success and the triumph over tragedy, but right then, Donnie Amos became nothing more to me than a competitor lining up to kick an extra point that would erase our lead.

The ball was hiked to their holder who caught it cleanly and set it on the tee. Donnie Amos approached the ball just as our defensive end, the very player who had suggested we should take it easy on their kicker, broke through the line, streaked toward the ball, and dove to block the kick.

Donnie Amos swung his leg and made contact with the ball, and it rose from the tee and grazed the outstretched fingertips of our defensive end. The ball wobbled and spun wildly, having been partially blocked. It struck the left upright on the goalpost and bounded through.

The Granite Ridge fans went wild as the game was, once again, tied.

Bradley Hope raced onto the edge of the field and embraced the defensive end that had given a maximum effort to block the extra-point kick.

Hope shouted, "That was great!"

The defensive end patted Hope on the back and replied, "Hope, that was all about you. I wouldn't have gotten close to it except for what you said."

I was proud of our defensive end, proud of Donnie Amos, and most proud of Bradley Hope, but the fact remained we were in a tie game with our rivals, and we needed a win to secure our place in the playoffs.

Great players and great people always rise to the occasion. We took Granite Ridge's kickoff, and our return man ran it back to the 30-yard-line. Our quarterback, Jessie Hunter, led our offense onto the field and huddled 70 yards from the goal line.

I remember there were less than three minutes to go when Hunter took that first snap. He hit our tight end with a bullet pass right on the sideline. Our receiver caught the ball and stepped out of bounds to stop the clock. Then Hunter faked a handoff to our halfback and hit our split end with a 30-yard pass over the middle. It was a great catch, but our receiver couldn't get out of bounds, so I had to use our last time out to stop the clock.

Jessie Hunter came to the edge of the field, and I told him we only needed another 10 or 15 yards, then we would be in field goal range and could kick from there to win the game by three points.

Jessie Hunter shrugged, smiled, and confidently stated, "Yeah, Coach, we could do that, or I could just throw a touchdown pass here, and we could all go home."

Before I could say anything, he turned and jogged back onto the field, taking his place in the huddle.

Jessie Hunter took the next snap and dropped back for a pass. None of our people were open immediately, and it looked like Hunter was going to be sacked for a loss, but then he deftly eluded his would-be tacklers and fired a pass into the corner of the end zone, the likes of which I had not seen before nor since.

That single pass for a touchdown allowed us to win the game, but the media that was there to cover Donnie Amos gave that touchdown pass the coverage it deserved, which eventually resulted in Jessie Hunter having a great career as a college football player and even a couple of years in the NFL.

The fate of a game or a person's life can turn on a dime. A hopeful young man looking far into the future at the possibilities of life can be instantly left in the dark with one brief explosion; but then, through sheer force of will, he can defiantly turn the tables and emerge victorious.

The final gun sounded, and we won that game 34 to 27.

I shook hands with Coach Cline, but he pulled me into a brief embrace and said, "Thanks, Coach."

The players littered the field in groups of twos and threes congratulating one another.

I found Jessie Hunter talking to Donnie Amos with a group of reporters and cameramen gathered around.

As I approached, a reporter called, "Coach, that was a great play you called on the touchdown pass. Any comment?"

I glanced over at Jessie Hunter and smiled, answering, "You'll have to talk to my quarterback. I was just hoping to get a few more yards out of the drive and kick a field goal to win."

All of the cameras and microphones pointed toward Jessie Hunter.

As proud as I had been of Jessie Hunter when he had thrown that amazing touchdown pass to win the game, I was even more proud of him when he put his arm around Donnie Amos, looked directly into the television camera, and stated, "I knew we needed a touchdown because if we had kicked a field goal, they had enough time to bring the ball back down the field, and I knew that the Granite Ridge Giants have a great field goal kicker."

One of the reporters asked me if I had any comment about Donnie Amos. I told the reporter that, as their coach, I was proud of my team, but I also admired the performance of Donnie Amos. I left that reporter with a quote from Harry S. Truman himself.

"Brave men don't belong to any one country."

Chapter Thirteen

HEROES AND HEROICS

"Actions are the seeds of fate.
Deeds grow into destiny."
—HARRY S. TRUMAN

13

EXCITEMENT AND ENTHUSIASM WERE AT A FEVER PITCH THAT NEXT week at Truman High. Having beaten our rivals, the Granite Ridge Giants, and having qualified for the playoffs, it was just a matter of building on our winning record so we could get a good position and keep home field advantage in the post season.

Bradley Hope and Gina seemed inseparable and were seen together everywhere around the school.

I had stayed in touch with Coach Stockton and had actually gone to the hospital several times to check on Steve Gaylord, but there was no progress yet. They had him propped up in bed. He was alert and talking but still had no movement throughout his body.

I ran into Sister Mary Florene in the hospital elevator, and she assured me confidently all we needed to do was "keep the faith." Sometimes, that's not easy to do.

We had a pep rally scheduled that Thursday which was the day before our game with the Carlton Red Hawks. It was homecoming week, which meant a lot of extra activities and fanfare surrounding our game, and I had just learned that Latrelle Johnston would be back at Truman High, along with his classmates and teammates, celebrating their 10-year reunion. If there's a true, enduring hero in Springfield, and certainly at Truman High, it would be Latrelle Johnston. He was several years ahead of me in school and had graduated before I began high school, but he had made his mark in a big way on our school and, particularly, the football team.

He was already a giant in high school. Even his first year on the Truman Eagles, it seemed like he was a man competing with boys.

His junior year, he was a high school All-American, and by his senior year, Latrelle Johnston was recruited by every major college football program across the country. He had a stellar career at our state university and was drafted in the second round to play in the NFL.

As fate would have it, his team had a bye week on their schedule during our homecoming game. He called me early in that week. I will never forget answering the phone, and he said, "Coach Fullerton, my name is Latrelle Johnston, and I graduated from Truman High."

I laughed aloud, and he asked, "Did I say something wrong, Coach?"

"No," I assured him. "It's just that having you call to introduce yourself and tell me who you are is like the President of the United States calling the White House and identifying himself like he was a stranger."

He went on to explain that since his team had the week off, he would be flying in on Thursday for his class reunion events and the homecoming game, and he would be staying through the weekend.

I told him about the pep rally Thursday and let him know I would expect him to say a few words there and, hopefully, speak to our team before the game.

He humbly and reluctantly agreed.

Thursday morning, I was at school early and stopped by to pay my respects to President Truman. I thought about his grace and humility which put me in mind of Latrelle Johnston.

One of Harry's best quotes came to mind. "Conceit is God's gift to little men."

That afternoon at the pep rally, I introduced our team and then let everyone know we had a special guest. I had tried to keep Latrelle Johnston's presence in the school and his appearance at the pep rally a secret, but it's not easy to keep a 6-foot-6, 320-pound man hidden and under wraps.

Everyone went wild when I introduced Latrelle Johnston and brought him to the podium.

He humbly thanked me—along with the rest of the faculty, staff, and student body—for welcoming him back to Truman High. He shared some of his fondest high school memories along with some of the lessons he had learned when he was a student.

He told the kids that, when he had been at Truman, he thought he knew it all, but he explained life had taught him he had a long way to go as an athlete and a person.

Then Latrelle Johnston shared a quote from Harry Truman. "It's what you learn after you know it all that counts."

Everyone laughed heartily, but I could tell from all the expressions left on a number of faces that Latrelle Johnston was having an impact.

At the end of the pep rally, the principal thanked everyone and instructed the students to return to their fifth hour classes.

I was seated at my desk as my students were filing into the classroom for U.S. History when an alarm sounded that I had hoped I would never hear. That particular ring indicated that there was a terrorist alert, and I should get my kids out of the school building as quickly as possible.

I instructed the kids to stay together and follow me, and we went out the nearest exit and rushed onto the parking lot. I lined up my students and counted them to make sure everyone was present and accounted for, and I could see the other teachers doing the same thing as fire trucks, police cars, and emergency vehicles arrived and surrounded the school building.

I was relieved when I reconfirmed that I had 31 students, which accounted for everyone in my fifth hour class. I told everyone to stay put, and I rushed over to the principal to try to get some details and further instructions.

The principal was talking to the chief of police as I walked up. Apparently someone had called in a potential terrorist threat and claimed that there was a canister of poison gas that was going to be released into the school building.

As I stood there trying to grasp the reality of the situation and determine how best to protect my students, our science teacher rushed over to us and explained breathlessly, "I think it's Troy Fisk... He got to my class late, and he was acting weird. When the alarm sounded, he was running down the hall the other way holding a gas canister from the lab."

The chief of police asked, "Are there any poison gases in your lab?"

The science teacher responded, "No, but I have no idea what's in that canister."

The chief instructed his officers to move everyone back further from the building and try to confirm that all the students had gotten out.

A SWAT team began donning their emergency gear and dispatching sharpshooters around our school building. It looked like a war zone and felt like a disaster waiting to happen.

The school counselor rushed over to us and exclaimed, "I'm in charge of study hall this hour, and everyone's here except for Troy Fisk. He's missing."

Troy Fisk had never been in any of my classes, but I had seen him around school. He seemed to be a loner and a bit odd. His name had come up in several of our faculty meetings as someone to keep an eye on.

Then my heart stopped when I heard somebody yell, "Bradley, stop… Don't go in there."

I whirled in time to see Bradley Hope sprint across the school lawn and duck into the side door of the school building.

The chief said in frustration, "It's bad enough to have a terrorist threat without having a hostage crisis."

He looked at all the teachers and counselors around him and asked, "Does anybody know that kid?"

I stepped forward and spoke, "Chief, Bradley Hope is a great kid with a good head on his shoulders. Whatever happens, I know that he's only trying to help the situation."

The chief got on his radio and informed all of the police personnel and the SWAT team that there was a second target or potential hostage in the building. The tension built as I looked at the angry weapons covering the school building from every angle.

The chief of police and our principal began to implement a strategy that would allow the hostage negotiator to talk on the school's public address system. Time seemed to stand still as everyone held their breath. The hostage negotiator spoke on a microphone calmly encouraging Troy Fisk and Bradley Hope to come out of the building, but his repeated instructions seemed to be ignored.

Just as the SWAT team captain was preparing his men to rush the building and secure it, one of the front doors to the building slowly began to open. Guns were trained on the door as it opened wider, and I saw Bradley Hope emerge, waving his right arm, and he had his left arm around the shoulders of Troy Fisk. Bradley was shouting for everyone to hold their fire while Troy Fisk cried uncontrollably.

The SWAT team surrounded the two and patted them down to make sure the danger had passed.

They led Bradley and Troy Fisk toward the emergency vehicles, and I could hear Bradley explaining, "He opened the valve on the canister a few minutes before I got him to walk out with me."

The paramedics began taking vital signs from the two boys as they rushed them toward the ambulances.

I was standing next to the chief of police as they put Bradley Hope onto a gurney and slid him into the back of an ambulance.

The chief of police said, "Son, you could have been killed. Do you have some kind of death wish?"

Bradley looked directly into my eyes and said, "You explain it to him, Coach."

They slammed the ambulance doors and sped away.

Classes were dismissed and activities cancelled for the rest of that day at Truman High School, but even so, I had to stay to be sure that all of my students were safe and secure until they were picked up by parents or left in their own vehicles. It was several hours before I was able to make my way to the regional hospital to check on Bradley Hope.

As I rushed into the hospital, I spotted Dr. Ryan standing at the nurse's station, and I hurried over to him blurting, "Bradley Hope?"

He nodded a greeting at me and announced, "Coach, we ran a lot of tests, and the gas was harmless."

I exhaled a long sigh of relief, but noticed that the doctor still seemed distressed.

I asked, "Is there something else?"

He nodded and signaled for me to walk with him saying, "One of the blood tests we did on Bradley to screen for toxins in the gas revealed an extremely elevated cancer marker."

I was stunned and protested, "Doc, I thought he was safe and out of the woods for a while at least."

The doctor nodded and replied, "Me, too. We're going to have to keep him here for a while and get on top of this."

He turned to push open the door of a hospital room and said, "Coach, you're going to have to excuse me. I'm spread a little thin here."

Dr. Ryan disappeared inside the hospital room, and the door eased closed behind him.

I wandered aimlessly back down the hospital corridor and then noticed a familiar face approaching.

Sister Mary Florene exclaimed, "Coach, are you ready for a new assistant coach yet?"

I replied distractedly, "Sister, Bradley Hope—"

She interrupted, "Yes, I know all about it."

We walked and talked, and I expressed my frustration asking, "So, Sister, what are you supposed to do when everything seems to be slipping away in spite of your best effort?"

She answered reassuringly, "Coach, there's always something to be done for someone somewhere."

I was just getting ready to tell her how absurd that statement sounded when we rounded the corner and spotted Gina and Bradley Hope's mother sitting on a bench holding hands.

Sister Mary Florene patted me on the back and whispered, "Coach, I'll leave you to do what needs to be done."

Chapter Fourteen

PAIN AND RECOVERY

*"We must have strong minds, ready
to accept facts as they are."*
—Harry S. Truman

14

I SAT WITH MRS. HOPE AND GINA LATE INTO THE EVENING. WE laughed and cried as we shared our thoughts and memories of Bradley. I was struck by the fact that we each loved and appreciated the same young man in our own ways and from unique perspectives.

Eventually, Dr. Ryan came out to tell us that Bradley was sleeping, and there wasn't going to be anything else going on that night, so he encouraged us to go home and get some rest.

I walked with Mrs. Hope and Gina to the parking lot and did my best to be a source of strength and encouragement for both of them.

I knew I wouldn't be able to get to sleep that night so instead of going straight home, I stopped off to visit with Harry. I sat on the bench, and I thought about all the challenges and crises that Harry had faced throughout his life.

There had been an assassination attempt on Harry's life. While he was never in immediate danger, one of the agents that had been on duty to protect him got killed. I knew that event had to weigh on Harry for the rest of his life.

I thought about his decision to drop the atomic bomb resulting in unimaginable death and destruction. I remembered his statement, "Once a decision was made, I didn't worry about it afterward."

We won our final three regular season games quite handily. The last game of the year is always senior day, and we dedicate the game to the young men who would be graduating.

Bradley remained in the hospital and had to undergo some pretty dramatic treatments to slow the progress of his aggressive cancer. He had wanted to keep his condition a secret, but that became impossible during his prolonged hospitalization.

I stopped in to see Bradley virtually every day. He seemed to be shrinking before my eyes as the treatment took its toll on healthy cells as well as the cancer cells. His hair began falling out in clumps, so eventually he just shaved his head to make life simpler.

I dropped by to see him after our final regular season victory and senior day. Our team had voted, and the school board approved the Truman Eagles retiring Bradley's jersey at the end of the season. In the long and storied history of Harry S. Truman High, the only Eagle who had ever had his number retired was Latrelle Johnston.

Tears ran down Bradley Hope's face as I told him that his jersey would be displayed in our trophy case in the main hall next to Latrelle Johnston's.

Dr. Ryan stuck his head into the hospital room as I was presenting Bradley with a plaque commemorating the honor.

The doctor blurted, "I'm sorry, Coach. I can come back after you make your presentation."

I motioned him into the room and declared, "Doctor, please join us."

Dr. Ryan stood on one side of Bradley's bed, and I stood on the other holding the plaque out in front of him, declaring that, due to a unanimous vote of his teammates and approval of the school board, his jersey would be retired.

Bradley wiped the tears from his eyes and said, "Thanks, Coach, but...Latrelle Johnston was an All-American who played at the state university and in the NFL. I wasn't even able to play in one game this whole year."

Sometimes, as a teacher or coach, you hope you can share the right words at the right moment because you know a vulnerable young person is at a crossroads in life. I heard myself saying the words I hoped would come.

"Son, Latrelle Johnston was a great ballplayer who brought us many touchdowns and a lot of wins. You are a great person who brought us a lot of enthusiasm, courage, and hope."

Bradley nodded and spoke. "Thanks, Coach, but does the fact that you are retiring my jersey mean I won't be able to suit up for the playoffs?"

I paused and explained, "Son, that's not a coaching decision."

Bradley and I both looked at Dr. Ryan.

He said thoughtfully, "Well, you're going to be in here another week or two. If the playoffs go beyond that, we'll have to see."

Before the first game of the playoffs began, I stood in the locker room and confronted my team.

I said, "Congratulations on a great season and making it to the playoffs. We've had a very good year. It's a mistake in football or in life to accept *very good* when *great* is available. A lot of teams set their preseason goal to have a good record or make the play-offs. We've done that, but if you'll remember, our goal was to win the state championship."

The Truman Eagles clapped, cheered, and shouted their approval. When the locker room fell silent again, I continued.

"Winning a state championship is a worthy goal by itself. Every team starts out the year wanting to win the big prize, but only one team makes it. That should be enough motivation for anyone, but if you need a little bit more, I want you to think about your teammate, Bradley Hope. When I stood by his hospital bed to present him with the plaque and to tell him we were going to retire his jersey, the only thing he wanted to do was to be able to suit up and be with you guys."

I looked around the room at the faces displaying emotion and determination.

I concluded, "Gentlemen, the doctor tells me Bradley Hope won't be able to join us for at least a couple of weeks, so we've got to win this game to give him a chance."

Great players and great people will do things for others that they wouldn't do for themselves. In that first round of the playoffs, the Truman Eagles were, quite simply, dominant. They were excited to be participating in the playoffs; they were motivated by the potential of a state championship; but they were driven to give Bradley Hope the chance to suit up as a Truman Eagle one last time.

The day after our first-round victory in the playoffs, I went to the hospital to visit Bradley Hope and share the victory with him. As I pushed the door to his hospital room open, it was immediately evident that his bed was empty, and there was a hospital orderly cleaning the room.

I blurted, "Where's Bradley Hope?"

She shook her head and pointed up.

I fought off the immediate panic and asked, "What do you mean?"

English was obviously not her first language, but she walked with me into the hall and pointed to the stairwell. She finally made me understand that Bradley, for some reason, was on the floor above us.

I took the stairs two at a time and rushed into the corridor of the floor above Bradley's room. I hurried over to the information desk and inquired, "Bradley Hope?"

A nurse smiled and pointed to the far end of the corridor explaining, "They should be coming around that far corner any minute."

Nothing made sense to me, and I blurted, "They?"

The nurse just smiled and nodded, and I began walking down the corridor in the direction she had indicated. Just then, I spotted Bradley Hope walking around the corner with his arm around Gina who was helping to support him. Then I was even more shocked as another figure rounded the corner who was on the other side of Gina. She was also helping to support him.

I rushed toward the trio, and as I got close I realized the third figure was Steve Gaylord. He was weak and unsteady but walking nonetheless.

I was filled with joy and relief and called, "Gina, this confirms one of my theories that cheerleaders are better athletes than football players. I've always believed that, but watching you carry these two guys settles the matter once and for all."

That Friday, we played in the last round of the playoffs before the state championship. One more win, and we would be in the big game.

We were playing the Stanton Stallions. While we had one player who had a potential college football career ahead of him, Stanton had four or five young men on their team who could play at the next level. In football coaching terms, they were loaded.

If you just looked at the two teams on paper, we didn't have a chance, but as old Coach Bartlett said, "We don't play football games on paper."

The Truman Eagles ran onto the field, and the crowd went wild.

The team huddled around me for a final word before kickoff. I thanked them for a great season and reminded them to do their best, have fun, and play with no regrets.

I was ready to deliver my final word when Jessie Hunter interrupted.

"Coach, if you don't mind, I'd like to say something."

If anybody had earned the right to speak and deliver the last word, it was Jessie.

I nodded and said, "Son, you wrap it up, and let's kick this thing off."

Jessie looked around the huddle and made eye contact with each of his teammates. Then he slowly thrust his hand into the middle of the circle and declared, "For Bradley Hope."

The other players all joined hands in the middle of the circle and thundered, "For Bradley Hope!"

As I look back on it from the perspective of several decades, I would have to admit that the Stanton Stallions were a far better team than we were that year. If we had played 10 times, I'm certain they would have won nine of the games, but that night, they didn't have a chance. The Stallions were playing for a chance to be in the state championship game while the Truman Eagles were playing for a special teammate. They had talent, but we had Hope.

When the final gun sounded, I looked up at the scoreboard which proclaimed Truman Eagles 35, Stanton Stallions 17.

We were going to the championship game.

Over the next few days, I met several times with Dr. Ryan, and he finally agreed that Bradley Hope could get out of the hospital Wednesday, attend our practice on Thursday, and suit up for the championship game Friday night.

Dr. Ryan warned, "Coach, this is against my better judgment."

The silence stretched out between us as we both weighed the reality and the possibilities of the situation.

Bradley came to school that Thursday and met with me in my office before practice. He was wearing a Truman Eagles baseball cap on his bald head.

He confessed, "Coach, I'm sort of embarrassed about not having any hair."

I considered the appropriate response, then demonstrated the confidence I had in a special young lady, asking, "What does Gina think about it?"

He laughed and responded, "She thinks it's cool and said I should keep it this way."

I smiled and stated emphatically, "Son, that's all that needs to be said."

The other players were on the field warming up when Bradley Hope and I made our way across the parking lot toward the stadium. He was frail and weak, so I walked slowly.

When we arrived on the sideline, Jessie Hunter jogged over to join us. The two players shook hands warmly. I thought Jessie was going to say something on behalf of the team, but he just stepped back, took off his helmet, and revealed his own shaved head. On cue, every player on the field pulled off their helmets revealing the fact that every player on my team had shaved their heads in tribute to Bradley Hope.

I stood there with my mouth open in stunned silence. You try to teach your players solid principles and train them to do the right thing, but sometimes they exceed your expectations.

Jessie Hunter looked at me and explained, "Coach, we took a vote, and I didn't think you'd mind, but for the championship game, we're the Bald Eagles."

Chapter Fifteen

ENDINGS AND BEYOND

"Human life is something that comes to us from beyond this world. The purpose of our society is to cherish it and to enable the individual to attain the highest achievement of which he is capable."
—HARRY S. TRUMAN

15

The high school championship game was to be held at the state university stadium a few miles from our state capitol. My boys were used to playing in high school stadiums in small towns scattered throughout our part of the state, but they had never seen anything like the immense edifice where they would be playing that night. The locker room, the field, and the entire stadium was a shrine to big-time college football.

The Truman Eagles were trying to remain calm and avoid shock and awe as we went through our pregame routine.

We were playing the Capital Metro Rams. This would be virtually a home game for them, as their high school was just a few miles across the city from the university.

I was proud that several thousand Truman Eagles fans had made the three-hour road trip to the state championship game to cheer on our team, but the majority of the stadium was filled with Ram fans.

There was a lot of hype and media coverage surrounding the state championship game. Our team got to meet the governor, the state university president, and their head football coach who greeted Jessie Hunter warmly and declared, "You show 'em what you can do tonight, son, and then we'll look forward to having you back here with us next fall."

Our pregame locker room was silent and tense. One of the dangers in preparing a team mentally for a big football game is that they get too keyed up and worried about making mistakes. You want your team to be striving to win instead of trying not to lose.

At the appropriate moment, I called for attention and told the Eagles to gather around.

I asked, "Well, gentlemen, are we having fun yet?"

I could hear laughter throughout the locker room and felt the tension beginning to drain away. I continued, "I went up to the press box for some TV interviews while you guys were warming up on the field. Looking down at all of your bald heads outlined against the green artificial turf, you guys looked like pool balls scattered across a billiard table."

The tension had broken, and hearty laughter echoed throughout the locker room.

I continued, "I'm really proud of each and every one of you. You have exceeded everyone's expectations, but not mine. You can win this game."

I looked at my boys and felt the pride in my chest and a lump in my throat.

I nodded to Jessie Hunter and declared, "Son, the final word is yours."

He nodded his thanks but pointed to Bradley Hope.

I shrugged and said, "Hope, we're all proud and pleased to have you with us. We're a team, and if there's even one guy missing, it's not the same."

I looked at Bradley Hope, smiled, and announced, "Son, I guess the final word is yours tonight."

Bradley stood up slowly, looking frail as if he'd shrunk inside his uniform which hung loosely on him.

He cleared his throat and said, "Thank you all for keeping the season alive until I could get back here with you, but it doesn't mean a thing if we don't win this game."

The Truman High Eagles roared their approval and took the field.

The Capital Metro Rams were a well-coached, well-disciplined group of superior athletes. They proved to everyone that they deserved to be in the state championship game, but so did we. The game went back and forth, and we were tied 17 to 17 at halftime.

The boys were much more relaxed and loose in the halftime locker room than they had been during pregame.

Before we went out for our last half of football that year, I proclaimed, "Gentlemen, you will look back on tonight for the rest of your life. You will tell your grandkids about the night you played in the state championship game. Many thousands of young men across the state started practicing football in August, and they all dreamed of being here tonight, but you are the ones who made it. For the rest of this game and for the rest of your life, always give it your all, and leave your best out on the field. You never want to be one of those sad souls who goes through life wondering *what if.* Now go out there, give it your best, because your best is always good enough, and I'll always be proud of every one of you."

The game seesawed back and forth, and in the fourth quarter, we kicked a field goal to take a two-point lead. I was excited to be on top, but knew that we had to kick off to them, and the two minutes left on the clock was more than enough time for them to get in field-goal range for their own kick to win the game.

They quickly moved the ball to midfield and needed about 25 yards more to give their kicker a chance to win the state championship for the Capital Metro Rams.

Their quarterback rolled out and threw a long pass to their receiver near the sidelines. Our safety leapt high, committing to the ball instead of defending the receiver. At the last instant, he batted the ball away from the receiver and was able to somehow catch it before he fell to the turf.

We had intercepted the pass and had the ball with a little over a minute to go.

The Truman Eagle fans jumped and screamed and cheered. We were going to win a state championship.

Our offense took the field except for Jessie Hunter who always stood next to me for last-minute instructions before he rushed out to call the play in the huddle.

I barked, "Son, all you've got to do is handle the snap, take a knee a couple of times, let the clock run out, and we win."

He nodded in understanding but just stood there.

I prompted, "Well?"

He pointed at the bench and explained, "Coach, I'd like to take Hope out there with me."

Tears sprang to my eyes, and I just nodded.

The Eagles bench erupted in shouts and cheers as Bradley Hope put on his helmet and stepped onto a football field for the first time during a game that season.

As Jessie Hunter and Bradley Hope jogged together toward the huddle, the stadium erupted. It wasn't only the Eagle fans cheering for Bradley Hope taking the field, but there had been so many media stories about Hope that the Rams' fans gave him a thunderous standing ovation.

As excited as I was to be a part of that special moment, I knew we still had a game to win, and it would take three plays to run out the clock.

The referee approached me as I was standing on the sideline. He and I had disagreed vehemently on several of his calls, and we had been in more than one shouting match that evening.

As he stopped in front of me, I queried, "What is it this time?"

The ref turned and looked at Jessie Hunter and Bradley Hope stepping into the huddle with the whole stadium around us in a prolonged standing ovation.

The referee answered, "Coach, I just thought that young man needed this special moment for as long as possible, so you and I are going to stand here and act like we're talking."

I smiled and replied, "Ref, you may not be as big a jerk as I thought you were."

He laughed and replied, "Well, Coach, it's possible you're not as big a jerk as I thought *you* were."

The thunderous ovation rolled on and on as play on the field resumed. Jessie Hunter took the first down snap from the center on our own 20-yard-line, stepped back, and kneeled to the ground as the clock continued to run.

We repeated the play on second down, and it was third down and 14 yards to go on our own 16-yard-line with under 30 seconds remaining.

The celebration had already begun on our sideline and throughout the stadium. We needed only one more kneel-down play to wind the clock down to zero.

Jessie Hunter stood over the center, confidently took the snap, and began to step backward; but before he could kneel down to end the game, the unthinkable happened. Somehow the ball was out and bouncing crazily along the turf.

I was stunned.

We had fumbled the ball deep in our own territory with just seconds to go in the state championship game. If Capital Metro recovered that fumble, they could easily kick a field goal to steal the victory from us.

It was a frantic scramble among the biggest, fastest, strongest football players in the state to recover that football.

Although I've watched game film of that single play a thousand times over the ensuing years, I still don't know how it happened, but somehow in the midst of that epic struggle, at the last split second, the smallest, slowest, and weakest player on the field fell on the loose ball.

Bradley Hope had somehow recovered the football. He lay there on the field cradling the ball for an instant when more than a ton of football players from both teams landed on top of him—all of them clawing and scrambling for the football.

A collective gasp could be heard throughout the stadium. Then everyone held their breath.

As the referees untangled the players one by one, they finally uncovered the bottom of the pile, and Bradley Hope was still lying there clutching the football, but he wasn't moving. Bradley Hope lay motionless on the turf holding the football.

I remember sprinting onto the field toward the crumpled, motionless form of Bradley Hope. Dr. Ryan, who had been watching the game from our sideline, matched me stride for stride, and we knelt down beside the emaciated, motionless body of Bradley Hope.

Dr. Ryan took his pulse quickly and then frantically signaled for the ambulance.

The emergency technicians quickly backed the ambulance onto the field, jumped out, and opened the back doors. They slid out the stretcher and set it on the ground beside Bradley Hope.

Dr. Ryan instructed, "Okay, let's get him onto the stretcher carefully without moving his neck or back."

One of the ambulance attendants cried frantically, "This kid won't let go of the ball."

Dr. Ryan calmly stated, "Just put him on the stretcher with the ball. Let's go."

Dr. Ryan jumped into the back of the ambulance and called to me. "Coach, we'll be at Capitol Heights Hospital."

The ambulance doors were closed, and they sped away.

The next few moments were a blur. I told one of our assistant coaches to take care of all the postgame activities, get all the boys on the bus, and head home for Springfield. One of our fans saw me running out of the stadium and offered to give me a ride to the hospital.

The first person I saw at Capitol Heights Hospital was Sister Mary Florene.

She motioned to me and called, "You need to come this way."

As we hurried down the hall, I observed, "Sister, this isn't your hospital."

She explained, "No, I just happened to be in town."

I was curious and asked, "What are you doing in town, Sister?"

She looked at me as if I had lost my mind and answered, "Well, you might have heard about it, Coach. There was this football game."

We shared a brief but welcome moment of laughter.

As we burst into the emergency room, an efficient woman at the desk told us Bradley was with the doctors now, and someone would be out to talk with us shortly.

Just as Sister Mary Florene and I were about to sit down, we saw Mrs. Hope and Gina enter the emergency room. I called to them, and they joined us. We cried, talked, and prayed a bit as we waited for some word on Bradley's condition.

A reporter approached and asked me my thoughts on winning the state championship. Ironically, I had forgotten all about it. The highest point in my professional career felt like the lowest point in my life.

I told the reporter, "We're waiting to hear from a doctor so we can find out if we won anything tonight or not."

Finally, Dr. Ryan emerged from a door down the hall and spotted us. Without any greeting or preamble, he laid it out.

"Bradley has a broken rib that has punctured his right lung. He's bleeding internally, and they're prepping him for surgery."

Mrs. Hope asked in a shaky voice, "Doctor, is he strong enough for major surgery?"

Dr. Ryan put his hand on Mrs. Hope's shoulder reassuringly and declared, "I was at the game tonight like everyone else. That's the strongest kid I've ever seen."

That was a long night. Bradley made it through the surgery, and after several hours in recovery, they got him into a hospital room. He was still unconscious and hooked up to a myriad of machines. He looked tiny and pale lying in the hospital bed.

Mrs. Hope, Gina, Sister Mary Florene, and I decided we couldn't sleep anyway, so we decided to stay with Bradley in the hospital room until he woke up.

Sometime before dawn, I must have nodded off, but when I jerked awake, I noticed Bradley's eyelids had fluttered. I rushed to his bedside. His eyes slowly opened, and he seemed to recognize me.

He croaked, "Coach, I didn't let go of the ball."

I laughed as a feeling of relief washed over me and replied, "No, son, you didn't let go of the ball. You held it throughout the ambulance ride, during the pre-op tests, and until they got you into the operating room. Only when you were under anesthesia could they get that football from you, and I think it still took two doctors and a nurse to do it."

Bradley's mother squeezed his hand, and Gina kissed him on the cheek as Sister Mary Florene whispered a prayer of gratitude.

Bradley looked back toward me and questioned, "The game?"

I spotted a newspaper that the orderly had delivered to the room. I picked it up, held it open, and let the headline speak for itself.

Hope Reigns. Truman Eagles Are Champs!

After several days at the hospital at the state capital, they transferred Bradley back to Springfield. A couple of weeks later, Bradley made it back to school in time for the ceremony to retire his jersey. The only other player to be so honored, Latrelle Johnston, flew in for the ceremony. As the two Truman Eagles stood side by side for photos, they looked like David and Goliath.

Bradley looked up at the NFL star and said, "It doesn't seem right. I wasn't an All-American, I won't play college football, and I certainly can't make it to the NFL."

Latrelle Johnston looked down at Bradley Hope, smiled, and stated, "Yeah, but I never won a state championship."

The two football heroes smiled, and the cameras clicked.

Bradley Hope completed his studies that spring and graduated with his class. Hope's fellow graduates voted not to have an outside commencement speaker but gave that honor to Bradley Hope instead. It was a day none of us will ever forget.

We lost Bradley Hope that summer. His funeral was the largest event anyone in Springfield could remember in our town.

Bradley would have been pleased, because we had to hold the service in the football stadium.

I went straight from the funeral to the first preseason practice for the new football year. I greeted my new team. I told them even though we were the defending state champs, we didn't have those players any more, and that team was gone. The only thing we would be taking into the new season from last year was Hope.

I proclaimed, "Gentlemen, sometimes when hope is all you have, it doesn't seem like much, but if you hold on tightly, it's enough."

I ended my reminiscing about that long-ago, shining season and gazed out again on that crowd that had gathered for my retirement banquet.

I told them, "Cancer took Bradley Hope's life, but it never took his dignity, his pride, or his hope. That is the championship tradition that flows through all of us here tonight."

I wiped a tear from my eye and continued as I told the crowd about a Benjamin Franklin quote that President Truman became very fond of as he was leaving the Oval Office and ending his presidency.

Franklin said, "In a free society, the rulers are the servants, and the people are their superiors and their sovereigns; and, therefore, for the former to return to the latter was not to degrade them, but was to promote them."

I continued, "So, ladies and gentlemen, I feel a bit like Harry Truman in that after 45 years as a Truman Eagle player, assistant coach, and coach, tonight I'm stepping aside as head coach, and I know someone else will take my place next year; but I'm not stepping aside as a Truman Eagle. I remain proud to be one of you as I move into the next phase of my life."

I took a worn piece of paper from my pocket and unfolded it as I continued, "Harry Truman was a fan of poetry. His favorite was a poem called "Locksley Hall" by Tennyson. Harry copied and recopied that poem dozens of times throughout his life just to keep up with the wear and tear on the paper. I've done the same thing for half a century. Harry did it with pen and ink, and thankfully, I had a Xerox machine."

The crowd laughed aloud. I smiled and pressed on.

"Tennyson wrote these words in the 19th century. They spoke to Harry Truman in the 20th century, and I hope they can guide us in the 21st century. I'll read one brief stanza."

I read aloud from the paper I held before me.

> *"When the centuries behind me like a fruitful land reposed;*
> *"When I clung to all the present for the promise that it closed;*
> *"When I dipt into the future far as human eye could see;*
> *"Saw the Vision of the world and all*
> *the wonder that would be."*

As a thunderous standing ovation erupted all around me, I refolded that beloved poem, slipped it back into my pocket, and walked from the stage.

I greeted former players, students, colleagues, and friends well into the night. Eventually, I found myself alone in the deserted hall. I turned and looked one last time at the banner proclaiming the special night to honor me. I turned and walked out of the building.

As I approached the familiar statue of Harry Truman, I noticed two small figures seated on the bench. When I got close enough to see them in the dim light from the parking lot, they seemed vaguely familiar. There was a middle-aged, attractive woman and an older lady. They stood and motioned me over.

I greeted them. "Good evening, ladies."

The younger woman said, "Coach Fullerton, I'm Gina, and this is Mrs. Hope."

The three of us hugged, sat on the bench together, laughed, and cried. Eventually, I walked the two of them to their car, and we all promised to stay in touch.

As I walked back toward my own car, I stopped in front of the statue one last time and spoke. "Mr. President, thank you for a great ride all of these years. You've blazed the trail and showed me the way a million times, and I know somehow whatever the future holds, you'll still be right here when an old, retired football coach needs you."

As I drove off into the night, I heard the voice of Harry Truman proclaiming one of my favorite quotes of his.

"Fame is a vapor, popularity is an accident, riches take wings, those who cheer you today may curse you tomorrow, and only one thing endures—character."

About the Author

In spite of blindness, Jim Stovall has been a National Olympic weightlifting champion, a successful investment broker, the President of the Emmy Award-winning Narrative Television Network, and a highly sought after author and platform speaker. He is the author of 25 books, including the bestseller, *The Ultimate Gift*, which is now a major motion picture from 20th Century Fox starring James Garner and Abigail Breslin. Four of his other novels have also been made into major motion pictures.

Steve Forbes, president and CEO of *Forbes* magazine, says, "Jim Stovall is one of the most extraordinary men of our era."

For his work in making television accessible to our nation's 13 million blind and visually impaired people, the President's Committee on Equal Opportunity selected Jim Stovall as the Entrepreneur of the Year. Jim Stovall has been featured in *The Wall Street Journal*, *Forbes* magazine, *USA Today*, and has been seen on *Good Morning America, CNN,* and *CBS Evening News.* He was also chosen as the International Humanitarian of the Year, joining Jimmy Carter, Nancy Reagan, and Mother Teresa as recipients of this honor.

Jim Stovall can be reached at 918-627-1000 or Jim@JimStovall.com.

SOUND WISDOM BOOKS BY JIM STOVALL

The Millionaire Map

Wisdom for Winners